Joan McCormick 63

W9-DJF-853

Enchanted Caravan

STARLIGHT NOVELS

By DOROTHY GILMAN BUTTERS

Enchanted
Caravan

ILLUSTRATED BY JANET SMALLEY

GROSSET & DUNLAP, *Publisher*

NEW YORK

COPYRIGHT, 1949, DOROTHY GILMAN BUTTERS

Printed in the United States of America
By arrangement with Macrae Smith Company

for

J. BRUCE and ESSA GILMAN

Enchanted Caravan

THE sun had just risen and was throwing long cool
shadows over the road to Gallup Corners. There was not
a sign of life to be seen anywhere. The trees on Crescent
Mountain stood out clearly in the dawn, like tufts of
green wool with pale ravelings of gold along their
outer rims. But in the valley from which the road issued
the mist still moved sluggishly among the hollows, like a
ghost river that had nowhere to go.

In the big house on the hill overlooking Gallup
Corners, Jennie Margaret Peel stood before a wide bay

window and shivered. The checkerboard linoleum was cold to her bare feet and there was a draft from the hall that stirred the folds of her nightgown, but it was not from cold that Jennie Margaret trembled, for she was as hardy as a Vermont sapling.

"That's the road *he'll* come on," she announced stormily, and then because she received no answer she said loudly and fretfully, "Lucy, do wake up. Lucy, do you think he'll come *today?*"

There was a sudden movement from the gleaming white bed. "You woke me up," said Lucy flatly and not without resentment. "I was asleep and you woke me up." She regarded Jennie Margaret solemnly, like a heavy-lidded young owl.

Jennie Margaret pointed at the row of identical beds that marched the length of the room. "Everyone's gone," she contributed. "The bell rang five minutes ago. They're washing their faces."

Lucy's round cheeks paled but she did not move. "You're terrible," she cried. "You know I always sleep through the bell and what's more you let me. How can I win a gold star this month if I'm late to breakfast every morning?"

"You can't *eat* a gold star. You can't even wear a gold star," said Jennie Margaret distastefully. "I can't imagine why you want one so badly. Why," she added scornfully, "all it means is that you're a good *orphan.*"

"Sometimes I don't care for you at all, Jennie Margaret Peel," said Lucy. She nibbled absently at her fingernail, then, remembering that she was growing it

10

long like a movie star, she examined it anxiously, saw the damage had been done and bit it off like a young savage. "After all," she added crossly, "I can't help it if I have no parents. *You* have a father."

"*I* have a father!" With a last glance at the road outside Jennie Margaret turned indignantly to her friend. "What's the good of having a father if I must live all my life in an orphanage?"

With one abrupt movement she discarded her nightgown, tossed it to the floor and began pulling on the green uniform that marked her as a member of the Gallup Corners Home For Homeless Children. Lucy watched placidly, like a young Buddha swathed in sheets for although she yearned for the world of perfection that brought gold stars and acclaim she was lazy by nature, the last in bed and the last to arise. With more affection she said now, "Do you really believe he'll come today?"

Jennie Margaret considered this for a moment. With the removal of the voluminous nightgown it was apparent that she was thin and wiry, small for her age and intensely active, as the network of bandages upon her knees proved. Her face was slim and pointed, not at all pretty but nevertheless appealing, for the force of her personality revealed itself in the splendor of her eyes. It was not inconceivable that at twenty Jennie Margaret would have an extravagant if unconventional beauty. At the moment her eyes were defiant and cruel.

"I wish he'd never come," she said at last, with a triumphant smile.

11

Lucy stared at her reproachfully. "He's your father, Jen. How can you say a thing like that?"

"Ha," sniffed Jennie Margaret, "you *say* he is, but how do you know? It's quite possible that he's an . . . an *impostor.*"

Lucy was stunned. "You mean . . . ?"

Jennie Margaret nodded. "It may be a plot, a smooth, slick move. But anyway," she added uneasily, "what makes him come here? I'm almost fourteen years old now and I've never seen him. Why does he come?"

"Maybe he's inherited a million dollars," suggested Lucy.

"It's more likely," said Jennie Margaret darkly, "that I have." She raised her chin angrily. "I may be a princess, you know, with a disinherited kingdom; or the heiress of millions and born to the . . . to the blue."

"Why, Jennie Margaret Peel, Miss Arbuckle says you were born right here in Gallup Corners and your father worked in the boiler rooms. So there."

"Well, you'd better get up," countered Jennie Margaret coldly, "there's knitting class right after breakfast." .

As she saw Lucy brighten and jump from bed her own movements slowed correspondingly for she intensely disliked knitting; it was difficult for her to sit still and pour all of her energy into ten fingers; then, too, the needles were slippery, no matter what kind she used, and she made so many mistakes that no one ever praised her as they did Lucy. But since reading *The Tale Of Two Cities* her attitude toward knitting had mellowed. Now

she liked to think of herself as a young Madame De-
Farge working beside the guillotine. In her mind she
had already beheaded several Board members of the
orphanage, the janitor's son who made pie-beds, and a
plump contemporary with long blonde curls.

"If he comes, if he should come," suggested Lucy,
banging bureau drawers, "will they tell him—about us,
I mean?"

"Of course they will," Jennie Margaret said gloomily.
"What else do they do all day long but think up beastly,
wicked ways to tease us? Horrid people."

"Oh, I don't know," Lucy remarked mildly, tying
knots in her hair ribbon. "Miss Arbuckle isn't so bad.
She gave me a chocolate bar yesterday and said I was
cute."

"Nuts," said Jennie Margaret, "it's just to trap you."

"Well," said Lucy, who had of late begun to develop
opinions of her own, "I still think she's nice. I'll bet she
won't tell your father how we ran away to the circus and
all."

"Nuts," murmured Jennie Margaret eloquently.

"And besides," continued the fair-minded Lucy, "you
said they'd boil us in oil when we got back, but they
didn't do that."

"Oh, for Heaven's sake," cried Jennie Margaret re-
belliously, "you don't have to be so *petty*. And they *will*
tell my father about the circus, they will, they will!"

Lucy opened her mouth to reply but they were both
silenced by the unmistakable sound of oxford heels upon
the floor outside.

"Jennie Margaret Peel?" called a voice from the hall, and as Jennie Margaret shrank against the wall the figure of Miss Arbuckle burst in upon them.

"Good morning, good morning," cried Miss Arbuckle. "Jennie Margaret, we've just received the great news. Your father will arrive this *morning,* not long after breakfast. Lucy, bring her along now, won't you? Oh, my dear, what a momentous day for you!"

"Yes," whispered Jennie Margaret sickly. "Oh, Lucy, whatever shall I do?"

"Why," said Lucy, smiling brightly at Miss Arbuckle, "brush your teeth and go to breakfast. Come along, Jen."

Jennie Margaret nodded. She stood up, testing her knees and just as she thought, they wobbled. Carefully placing one foot before the other, as if unsure of her strength, she walked to the door where Lucy and Miss Arbuckle awaited her patiently. She was, after all, only thirteen. Madame DeFarge had been well along in years.

IN the silence of a green tangle near the fork of the road to Gallup Corners, a mongrel hound stirred and cocked an ear. He sniffed ominously. There was something in the wind that stiffened the hairs of his flea-bitten old back and brought muffled growls to his throat. It was not the distant piping of the Boston milk train; the sounds carried to him the undertones of a personal invasion. Uneasily the mongrel rose to his feet.

Across the highway in the elbow of pines that groped toward the road another sleeping figure awakened, listened, and with quickening heart arose. With hasty fingers Mr. Herb Bowler of Brooklyn adjusted his tie and checked the lock of his briefcase. He combed his hair carefully with a comb from which several teeth were missing, and when the strands were firmly in place he

pushed the hair slightly forward with the flat of his hand
so as to encourage its faint wave. Then, his morning toi-
let completed, he set out for the road and whatever adventure the approaching sound might bring him. He had
not long to wait.

Over the hill from Lanesborough with the propulsion
of a comet released from an invisible slingshot, roared
a strange apparition of the road. It was a vehicle; a very
old, very dilapidated omnibus, bursting at its seams,
creaking in every joint, swaying madly and emitting
sounds of loud indignation. From its hood streamed a
flag; from its underpinnings roared the sounds of an
army. It was, clearly, a bus with a broken muffler.

Mr. Bowler's thumb lifted hopefully. Nearby, the
mongrel hound opened his mouth with a yelp of dismay
that was answered by a score of companion barks; from
every barn and doorstep poured dogs that had been bred
and born for just such an emergency. A cow mooed; a
horse neighed. Windows flew up and sleepy heads were
pushed out to protest this untimely invasion. The coun-
tryside was awake.

"Well," gasped a farmer's wife. "Well! What can it
be?"

"Look," shouted the farmer, "it's an old school bus!
Isn't it?" But his authority vanished in doubt.

"There aren't any seats inside," cried his young son.
"Only a machine, and shelves and things."

"And see," cried the farmer's wife, brushing the sleep
from her eyes, "there are curtains in three of the windows! I declare!"

"Well, now there," said her husband as the bus slowed to accommodate Mr. Bowler, "there's the answer, on the door. See the sign? 'Jeremy Peel's Caravan, Knives and Tools Sharpened.'"

"Aw," cried his son, "aw shucks, is that all!"

"Breakfast in half an hour," shrilled the wife, and slammed the window with a bang.

"Durn noisiest contraption I ever heard," muttered the farmer and went off to brush his teeth.

For Herb Bowler the approach of Jeremy Peel's Caravan also held impact. He ran his eyes admiringly over the silver paint, the scarlet lettering and the swelling bulge of its carriage. As the Caravan slowed to admit him a pleased smile creased his cheeks. Lowering his head he charged the running board, straightened, and with a little sigh dropped into the seat beside Jeremy Peel.

"Glad you made the jump," observed Jeremy Peel. "Bus stalls when I come to a full stop." His round bird-like eyes met Herb Bowler and withdrew, shyly. "Name's Peel," he volunteered. "Goin' to Gallup Corners if it's all right with you."

For a moment only the sound of Mr. Bowler's rapid breathing could be heard above the din. Then, "Yes, sir," he replied. "Mighty glad for the lift. The name is Bowler, Herbert A. Bowler from Brooklyn."

Unaware that his companion found it necessary to shout, Mr. Peel accelerated his Caravan with happy unconcern. He was a little man, almost shrunken as though from great age, but he was in truth only fifty. He had a

17

rich, pleasant mouth and a large nose with a great deal of character; his eyes had a tendency to look fierce but this was partly due to the lowness of his brows and partly because he was very shy. He wore a pair of unpressed trousers and a blue serge jacket. His shirt and tie matched exactly, which gave him a rakishly sporting appearance, not unlike a rabbit in wolf's clothing. Mr. Bowler thought he somewhat resembled a rabbit with his little round cheeks, large nose and bright eyes.

"You certainly don't need any brass bands to tell Gallup Corners you're coming," said Mr. Bowler kindly. "Bad muffler?"

Jeremy Peel blinked. "Stars and garters!" he exclaimed. "I forgot all about that muffler." His nose quivered suddenly as though it sniffed the air. "Very bad is it?" he inquired.

"Not very," returned Mr. Bowler generously. "Too bad I don't sell mufflers, though; this would be a real opportunity for me."

"Salesman, eh?" queried Jeremy. "What would your line be, Mr. Bowler?"

"Call me Herb," suggested the young man modestly. He hesitated. "I sell books. Only not just ordinary books, Mr. Peel." He leaned forward emphatically in his desire not to be misrepresented. His rough-hewn face took on a fervent glow. "No sir, I'm a missionary, that's what I am, Mr. Peel. I'm out to give the world what it needs."

"Well, really?" cried Jeremy with enthusiasm.

"I sleep in the open doing it," confided Mr. Bowler. "Live on peanuts, too—that's figurative, that is, not literal. I guess that makes me a real missionary, doesn't it?"

"Religious work?" hazarded Jeremy.

"Ha," cried Mr. Bowler, "that's the first thing comes to mind, isn't it. No sir, Mr. Peel, I serve the public not the church; the Great American Public, the Vast Body of People behind our Democratic Way of Life. What I'm selling," he divulged, shyly, "is knowledge."

"Knowledge, eh?" Jeremy was rather taken aback.

"Yes, sir. Now you might," continued Mr. Bowler, "think a salesman would give the People what they want and nothing more. That's what Mr. Average Salesman does, but not me, Mr. Peel, not me. You see, I got Plans, Great Plans. I'm a Man of Thought and a Man of Action, and this is the way I see it; why not sell the American People not just what they want but what they *need?*"

"Why, of course," replied Jeremy, dazzled.

"I like to think," went on Herb, "that I'll help shape the destinies of the American People, the Great Public which I'm planning to serve. Of course," he added sadly, "I'm only beginning. Been in the Army, you know."

Jeremy sighed and his sigh held both delight and envy. "I wish I'd been young enough for the War," he confided. "Don't know whether you'll believe this or not, but I tried to get into the Service myself. Seems a long time ago, that disappointment; they claimed I was too old. I'd have shown those Germans a thing or two, you bet." He nodded his head decisively, once up and once down. "What did you do in the War, Herb?"

"K.P. mostly," said Herb. "But that was only because

I happened to be in the Quartermaster Corps. I'd have been a hero most likely if they'd sent me anywhere but the Aleutians."

"Quite so." Jeremy nodded sagely. "Well, I can see you've got a big future ahead of you, boy. Not like me with my knife-sharpening business; there's not much money in this, you know.

"But," he added eagerly, "I've done other things. I've been around, boy, really around."

Mr. Bowler looked politely interested.

"For instance," Jeremy mentioned casually, "I've been a clown." Seeing that he had impressed his audience he took a deep breath and elaborated. Very seldom was he given the opportunity to contribute so abundantly to a conversation. "Yes, Mr. Bowler, a real clown in a circus. I can still do a masterful cartwheel and once I could juggle fifteen plates at one time. They said I was pretty good, said I was headed for the big time, they did. But of course," he added sorrowfully, "that was years ago." He brightened. "My wife was the star of the show; trapeze artist, she was, 'til the baby came. You know how babies are?"

"On the contrary," said Herb with firmness, "I'm not married."

"Well, of course you're not, of course. Too young to think of that, being a missionary and all."

"Doesn't your wife mind your traveling like this?" asked Herb, who had glimpsed Jeremy's Pennsylvania license plate.

"She's dead," returned Jeremy soberly. "Took the

heart right out of me, it did. I tried keeping the baby, but it wa'nt no good. So I left. Been drifting, just drifting 'til I found my Caravan."

"And the baby?" pursued Herb reluctantly.

A shadow crossed Mr. Peel's face. "She's right where I put her," he said. "It's why I'm comin' here to Gallup Corners. Jennie Margaret's been boarded here since her ma died and I haven't seen her for twelve years." He repeated despondently, "Not for twelve years."

"She a pretty kid?" asked Mr. Bowler.

"Pretty?" Mr. Peel brooded a moment. "I wouldn't know. I haven't," he repeated doggedly, "seen her for twelve years."

This seemed to end the matter, as indeed it did. There was a silence between the two men while they each thought of intimate things concerning only themselves and certainly not each other. Then Herb, remembering his mission, said brightly, "You care to buy one of my books, Mr. Peel?"

Jeremy was startled. "No, thanks. That is, you know how it is. What I mean is," he explained hastily, "I don't have much money."

"I suppose not," ruminated Herb gloomily.

They had reached the outskirts of Gallup Corners, population six thousand one hundred and nine, and the Alabaster County seat. They could see grocery stores now, and trim, elm-shaded bungalows. They passed the Trinity Methodist Church and the aging Trivoli Picture Palace. It had been a long time since Jeremy had traveled its pleasant rural streets, but he was not surprised to find that nothing had changed; the City Fathers resisted progress as spitefully as Vermont had eluded the New Deal.

"We're here. This is Gallup Corners," said Jeremy. "Where can I drop you? Just name your corner, Herb."

Herb roused himself. He leaned forward and watched the empty streets of the town roll past until he spied an all-night diner shaped like a loaf of bread and tidily wrapped up in blue.

"That's it," he said. "You leave me there and I'll be most grateful, Mr. Peel. I'll go in there and order me ham and eggs and coffee with toast and jam. We salesmen have to be careful about ulcers, you know. Care to stop with me?"

Warmed by such camaraderie of the road but stunned by the size of his friend's appetite, Jeremy could only shake his head. He was too conscious of his shrinking funds. "No, thanks, Herb," he said.

They wrung each others' hands appreciatively. "Best of luck to you, Herb."

"Thanks, Mr. Peel. Same to you."

Impulsively, Herb reached into his satchel. With one foot on the running board and one deep in the dust he groped among its contents and at last extracted Huxley's *Brave New World*. He looked it over carefully, risked a glance of appraisal at Mr. Peel and shaking his head brought out a blue-jacketed book entitled *How To Get Along With The Russians*. Gladly he thrust it into Jeremy's hands.

"Here," he said. "Cost you three dollars in any book

store. Read it with the compliments of Herbert A. Bowler. From me to you."

Before Jeremy could thank him, Herb had leaped from the running board. Straightening his shoulders he turned with exquisite military trimness and marched down the street as if to the beat of celestial drums.

Blinking, Jeremy looked at the book that was his. He had never before owned a book. He examined the gaudy cover, its pages and their print. Then, standing first on one foot and then the other he read the introduction; it seemed a very wise and important book. When he had finished the introduction he leafed through the pages quickly to see whether they contained any pictures, found none and tenderly placed the book under the front seat. Then he headed for Petrie's Garage, the muffler screaming the news of his arrival in Gallup Corners.

JEREMY found Petrie's Garage with little trouble; it held an impregnable position on the main street of Gallup Corners. Streaks of morning sunlight laid patterns across the seamed walls of the building, tipping the petrol tanks with gold and lending the structure a charm it did not deserve. A few signs, pinned at curious angles along the back fence, praised the merits of varying brands of cigarettes, cars and cough medicines. With his customary tact Jeremy parked the Caravan in the rear.

Order

Price

Author

Title

Teacher

Name

Name Joan McCormack

Teacher Mrs. Cole

Title Enchanted Caravan

Author Dorothy Butler Pub. G.D.

Price $1.50

Order first Pd.

Name

Teacher

Title

Author

Price

Order

Name Joan McCormick

Teacher Mrs. Cole

Title Enchanted Caravan

Author Dorothy Butler Pub. B.D.

Price $1.50

Order first Pd.

"She needs a new muffler," he announced to the man who strolled across the yard. "You Mr. Petrie?"

"That's the name," said the man, shrewdly examining both Jeremy and his Caravan. "Stranger in town?"

Jeremy nodded. "As I say, she needs a new muffler. If I could leave my bus here for a few hours while you fix her?"

Mr. Petrie's head shot up as though jerked by invisible strings.

"I . . . I have an errand in town," Jeremy faltered apologetically.

Petrie's brows were high and the corners of his mouth curled downward. He said, "This ain't no public parkin' lot. You leave that contraption here longer'n one hour and I got to charge you." He thrust out his underlip fiercely. "Everybody takes advantage of Harry Petrie. All the time people park here. It'll be fifty cents to leave your bus. And five dollars for the muffler."

Jeremy, cold and breakfastless, trembled under this sudden barrage. "I only wanted . . ."

"And there ain't another garage in Gallup Corners," spat out Mr. Petrie. "You'll have to take my terms. Your muffler'll be fixed when you come back. You can pay then."

Breathing heavily, Mr. Petrie turned and disappeared into the black shadows of the garage. Jeremy sighed; Mr. Petrie had given to him a faint memory of defeat, as did all aggressive, confident men. I might have risked a bit of swagger, he thought wistfully. Fifty cents to park is outrageous and he knows it. Reflecting upon the sourness of human nature and the smallness of his own courage Jeremy walked back to the Caravan. He was hungry and wanted breakfast; he was discouraged and needed solace.

Jeremy could never restrain the glow of pride and possession that warmed him when he entered the Caravan. It was his home and though it was smaller than most, this was compensated for by the fact that it traveled about with him.

The cabin of the bus was divided roughly into two sections by a plyboard partition high enough for privacy and yet low enough to allow Jeremy's right hand to know, in a manner of speaking, what his left hand was doing. Behind the low-slung wall, to the rear, lay his workshop, its small, clever machines sandwiched into a minimum of space. Here were litters of dust and wood shavings and a complete masculine indifference to both.

But not so in the heart of the Caravan, for this was Jeremy's home. It became evident at a glance that in planning it Jeremy had first consulted a number of home magazines, but where knowledge and research had failed, ingenuity had prompted a few rather remarkable developments.

Against the right wall Jeremy had built his bunk with its fashion-wise niche for radio and magazines. Along the plyboard partition of the far wall ran an asbestos shelf crammed full with pots and pans, an electric plate, a small oven, a toy sink and an infinitesimal icebox. Bright red curtains, echoed gaily at each window, ran the length of this shelf, partially concealing the score of canned goods and crockery stored beneath.

In the upper left corner, incongruous in this doll's house, stood an old-fashioned rocking chair; a plush footstool lay at its feet, like a ludicrous afterthought.

But the tiny folding screen that hid his equally small wardrobe was Jeremy's secret pride. On it, as tattered bits of his past, he had hung newspaper clippings and photographs: his wife's obituary notice, a high school group picture with an arrow pointing to Jeremy's near-obliterated face, and a publicity photograph of Mrs. Peel which showed her on the high trapeze and proved that she had an excellent figure. There was also a snapshot of Jennie Margaret, age six months, lying prone on a bear rug, and a beaming picture of Mr. Peel at Coney Island. The remaining space was filled in with Hollywood closeups, some of them in color.

But these were only the highlights of Jeremy's life, the memories among which he moved happily when alone. There were no monuments to the back street in Philadelphia where he was born, nor to the long quiet years when by day he attended an invalid mother and at night a host of rebellious furnaces and boilers. That was the manner in which Jeremy had lived until he was thirty; vicariously, never quite matching his dreams to reality, watching others grow fat and sleek with experience while the years wasted away leaving him no one but himself to depend on.

Then, at thirty two, he met Madeline De Perchon.

Jeremy thought Madeline the most beautiful woman in the world, and it was this perhaps more than anything else that led Madeline to return his affection. Madeline belonged to the golden, glamorous world of the big top, where the show always went on: she was a trapeze artist. It never mattered to Jeremy that she was a third-rate performer in a fly-by-night carnival; the smell of greasepaint and the blare of the circus band became as ecstasy to him. They were married when his invalid mother died, not as prophesied, but of sheer old age. It was because the circus had no boiler rooms but did need a tumbling man that Jeremy became a clown.

He was a fine clown; it was not improbable that he was born to be a clown, so splendid was his talent for making others laugh, he who was only learning to laugh himself. But the fates roughly intervened. It was in Gallup Corners, not long after Jennie Margaret's birth, that Madeline, who had dared the most perilous jumps into mid air, succumbed to a common cold. She died of pneumonia.

With the arrangements Jeremy made at the Gallup Corners orphanage, which took his money but gave him nothing of Jennie Margaret, Jeremy was not at all discontent; it was, in a way, surcease. He was as proud of his independence as a miser of his gold and there were moments when he felt his cup to be running over. He drifted from job to job until a Philadelphia auction and a stroke of good fortune provided him suddenly with a knife-sharpening Caravan. Now the misfortunes of the past lay behind him, but from them Jeremy had learned not to tempt the fates too sorely. If asked his remaining desires in life he would have replied that he hoped he might be allowed to keep his Caravan, perhaps even the ninety-six dollars he had accumulated in a Philadelphia bank, but he had not forgotten that life was bigger than he and apparently hard of hearing. He was prepared, resigned, in fact, to enjoy only the present; but in his heart, which had at some period in his life outgrown his mind, there lingered the desire to put his flesh-and-blood responsibilities in order before settling too firmly among his knife-sharpening machines and valued loneliness. It was this that brought him to Gallup Corners.

Happily alone now among his treasured possessions, Jeremy went to the icebox and brought out bacon, one egg and a pint of milk. He plugged in his Electro stove and drawing the curtains made himself a tidy breakfast.

But if his hands were busy his mind had approached a state of extreme agitation, for the dreaded moment had arrived. Jeremy was here at last in Gallup Corners and on the hill overlooking the town stood the orphanage where Jennie Margaret awaited him. She was thirteen years old now, able to talk and think, to demand love and affection from him and, worst of all, to exercise her will upon him. He could see that following this meeting he might no longer be allowed to act with the impersonal kindness of a distant father, but would be bound to Jennie Margaret by ties which insist that blood relationship share all and be all. In his thoughts he had

29

come to picture Jennie Margaret as a small copy of his own mother, who had kept him close by illness and iron determination. He was afraid.

"I don't even know what she looks like," he told himself, and stared hard at the baby picture across the cabin. It was too much to hope that she might resemble Madeline De Perchon, and he could only pray that she had not inherited his own features. "Stars and garters," he thought, "what shall I say to her? She didn't even know her ABC's when I knew her. What in tarnation does any father talk about?"

There was no one to answer him. Now that he was in Gallup Corners Jeremy was not at all sure why he had come. Cross and unhappy he rinsed his dishes and, gathering up the box of candy he had brought for Jennie Margaret, began his forced march to the orphanage.

JEREMY waited for Jennie Margaret in a room which did not lessen his discomfort. It was not unlike a mausoleum where at almost any moment a funeral service would begin. A heavy marble clock, supported by gilt cherubs, ticked ponderously on the mantel; white plaster statues in semi-nude attire leered at him from every corner and when Jeremy cleared his throat the empty shadows flung it back at him in reproach. He stood uneasily at the edge of the worn rug and prayed for the return of the startling, but wholly alive, **young woman** who had left him to this cheerless vault.

He scarcely heard her approach. The heavy drapes whispered sibilantly, a heel crunched on a bare patch of floor and Miss Arbuckle was in the room again. With her was a reluctant Jennie Margaret.

"Here we are," rejoiced Miss Arbuckle. "Kiss your daddy, dear. And Mr. Peel, Jennie Margaret is to show you every inch of our little home, just every inch, when you two have finished your little talk." She smiled coyly at Jeremy. "Oh, we have some gay times here, Mr. Peel; some gay times."

This time a door could be heard closing behind Miss Arbuckle.

"Would you care to sit down?" asked Jennie Margaret primly.

Jeremy lowered himself into a vast chair with a gargoyle at its back and carved claws upon the arms. With quick, shy glances he assured himself that twelve years in an orphanage had done his daughter no perceptible damage; there were no limbs missing and no apparent defects, but it gave him a start to find that Jennie Margaret was neither himself nor her mother but an individual in her own right.

"Well, Jennie Margaret," he began feebly, "they treat you all right here?"

"Yes, sir," said Jennie Margaret, staring at the floor.

"I'll bet you have lots of friends?"

Jennie Margaret raised her eyes and leveled a look of such scorn at Jeremy that it was his turn to glance away.

He felt uneasy, in need of help, preferably in the form of a man to whom he could talk sensibly, but his gaze inevitably returned to Jennie Margaret.

"What I mean is," Jeremy explained, "you have plenty of orange juice for breakfast? Good hearty meals?"

"Oh, yes."

"Doctors? Dentists?"

Jennie Margaret risked a glance of curiosity at her father. "Oh, yes, sir."

Jeremy sighed; this was worse than he imagined. He directed an angry glance around him, as though it were the surroundings that choked him. He seized his collar and tried to loosen it but he succeeded only in twisting his tie. With an exclamation he stood up.

"Nuts," he groaned. "Let's get out of here, you and me."

A gleam of interest softened Jennie Margaret's inscrutable gaze. "Nuts?" she echoed.

"Yes, I said nuts. Come along."

Jennie Margaret arose thoughtfully and followed him out into the sunlight. "*I* say nuts," she said, "and I'm the only one in the orphanage who says it. It's strange you should say it, too."

"Eh?" cried Jeremy.

"Well, why did you say nuts?"

"Why, stars and garters, child, it's because I'm scared to death. I guess that seems mighty queer to you, my being afraid of *you*."

A little smile struggled for supremacy on Jennie Margaret's lips; a moment or two and it won out. "Oh, no,"

she confided eagerly, "because I'm afraid of you, too."
She paused to stare searchingly at Jeremy; then, to complete her confession, she rushed on heedlessly. "I was afraid they'd tell you about me and Lucy running away. We went to the circus and—oh! now I've told you!"

She flinched, ready to repudiate the momentary intimacy, but Jeremy only smiled, never realizing the acid test to which he had been subjected.

"I guess you come right by that, Jennie Margaret," he said. "Your mother was a trapeze artist and your father was a clown in the circus once. Yes, sir, I was a pretty good clown, too."

Jennie Margaret stared at him with feverish excitement. "A clown, a real clown?" she cried. "Oh, tell me about it. Did you wear paint, and a little suit with ruffles?"

"Yes, and I had a polka-dot on the end of my nose, and big shoes and red lines here, and here, and here."

"And did you turn cartwheels? The clown I saw turned cartwheels."

Jeremy braced himself, then hurtled through the air in what was unquestionably a professional cartwheel. Jennie Margaret's eyes burned with delight; she clapped her hands together in approval.

"I'm going to be a trapeze artist when I grow up," she announced, a secret that she had not even shared with Lucy. "I'm going to wear tights and swing on the trapeze."

Jeremy turned to look at her with respect; could it be

that what Madeline De Perchon had given to him had somehow been transmitted to their child? Life was very strange at times. He grasped Jennie Margaret's hand in his.

"Tell me more about your circus trip," he said firmly.

They walked happily down the road, Jennie Margaret painting for him in vast detail the glories of her unauthorized journey to the fairgrounds. When she had finished, Jeremy showed her how to be a clown; he even put on a juggling performance for her with two empty soup cans they discovered along the road. Jennie Margaret thought it truly comical. He told her all about Madeline De Perchon, of their old friend Gigi who walked on stilts, and of all the dogs and seals and horses he had known in the circus.

"Father," said Jennie Margaret suddenly, using the word unconsciously for the first time, "will I have to grow up in the orphanage? Aren't you ever going to take me away to live with you?"

Jeremy squeezed her hand and dropped it. "I wish I could," he said slowly, and not quite sincerely. "But I'm not a money-making man, Jennie Margaret. I got me this Caravan now; I sharpen knives and tools for people, but it don't pay at all, just a quarter or fifty cents a job, and when I get through paying your board here there's not much left to live on."

"But you wouldn't have to pay my board if I weren't here," protested Jennie Margaret. "You'd save lots of money having me with you."

35

"Another mouth to feed," Jeremy reminded her solemnly. "Living's expensive nowadays. And besides, the Caravan . . ." But Jeremy did not continue.

"Why do you call it a Caravan?" demanded Jennie Margaret.

"Why, because I live in it and travel all about in it."

"All around? To different cities even? Like New Orleans and Miami and New York?"

"Not yet," said Jeremy, "but the Caravan held together pretty well this trip. It looks mighty promising. Always wanted to winter in Florida, I did."

"Oh, Father," cried Jennie Margaret, "take me with you. It's hateful here, honest it is. Take me with you!"

"Oh, my now," said Jeremy uneasily. "You're a big girl, Jennie Margaret. You got to go to school and grow up educated. It's no life for you runnin' around the country with an old man like me."

"I can cook, I can dust, I can sew," cried Jennie Margaret, fierce as a panther now. "And besides, school is closed for the summer. It's vacation, truly it is."

"No, no, Jennie, you wouldn't be happy with me."

"I would, I would," she cried. "Can't you understand how I hate it here? I'll hate *you* if you don't take me away from this horrid place."

And Jennie Margaret broke into wild sobs. "Besides," she whispered, "you're a circus clown. *You* ought to understand."

It was the tears that did it. Jeremy had known but two women in all of his life, yet they in turn had known his Achilles Heel. The shades of his mother, even of Made-

36

line De Perchon, rose up to halt him but Jeremy's heart had crumbled.

"All right there, Jennie Margaret," he sighed, clumsily stroking her hair. "I'll take you along with me. But only for the summer, do you hear? Only for a little while."

Jennie Margaret nodded blissfully. "Oh, yes, Father!" she cried. And then, "Oh, just wait 'til I tell Lucy!"

Once again life was flirting with Jeremy, beckoning him out of the shallows and into its broad flowing stream.

AT half-past four that afternoon Jeremy had already discovered that life with Jennie Margaret was to be exhausting if diverting. Their walk from the orphanage to the Caravan was punctuated by a dozen or more stops for window shopping and ultimately, just as day follows night, for actual shopping; Jeremy was pressed into seeing through Jennie Margaret's enraptured eyes the beauties offered in each new store. He succumbed at last to the desire to own a few of these breathtaking treasures so that, as they approached the Caravan, they carried small packages in their arms: a shaving mug, entirely necessary to them because of the pine tree sketched upon its patina, a charm bracelet with a scaly blue fish that moved limply, a flowered drinking glass, a gaudy jump rope, and a bright red rubber ball. Jeremy's budget was evaporating in a cloud of abandon.

Now Jeremy threw open the door of the Caravan with a grandiose gesture, for this was his moment; this which he had created was to be praised and shared.

"This is it, Jennie Margaret," he said.

"Why, it's big," Jennie Margaret cried happily, "it's a whole little house!"

He allowed her to slip past him, daring her to find it shabby or ridiculous. Jennie Margaret gave most of her attention to the radio, to the icebox, and the pictures of the movie stars, but she loved everything and to such excess that Jeremy was warmed into a benign happiness such as the Caravan alone had never given him. Carefully he placed the shaving mug and the drinking glass over the sink. He made room for Jennie Margaret's pajamas and her Sunday dress, her toothbrush and hair comb. With these acts it became *their* Caravan.

"Did you see Lucy cry?" asked Jennie Margaret with satisfaction. "She cried and kissed me good-bye. It's going to be nice being missed. I've never been away before, so nobody could ever miss me."

"Kinda hard on Lucy, isn't it?" observed Jeremy.

"Oh, yes. But that's part of the niceness. When Janie Palmer got adopted we all cried and cried. I think it's much easier to go away from people than be left behind."

Jeremy considered this, but since he had always been left behind he had no basis for a decision.

"Lucy and I slept together," Jennie Margaret continued. "She's pretty big for her age, and fat, too, but in the winter her feet are warm. Where shall I sleep, Father?"

They decided, for the meantime, that Jennie Margaret might sleep on the trunk behind the rocking chair. It was a close fit but when Jeremy demurred Jennie Margaret became firm; the orphanage was but a mile away and she intended there to be no last-minute change of plans. She remained adamant; the trunk was hers, and it was her problem to remain the same size all summer.

"We'll leave in a few minutes," said Jeremy, remembering the muffler. "You tend the Caravan while I see if she's been fixed up proper. I'll have to go up to the corner, too, and buy us some food for dinner."

But Jennie Margaret scarcely heard him, and she was certainly too busy exploring her new home to notice Jeremy's reluctance at leaving. She gave the rocking chair a loving pat in anticipation of many luxurious moments in it, and then flew across the room to test the springs of the bunk. But as she heard Jeremy poking about outside the Caravan she realized that soon they would be leaving and that she was very thirsty indeed.

"I wonder," she said, standing on one foot and looking around her.

But Jeremy had neglected to show her the jars of spring water in the cupboard under the sink. There was not a drop of liquid to be seen. With a sigh Jennie Margaret opened the door.

"Father?" she called, but Jeremy had already departed for the grocery store.

The garage was deserted. Jennie Margaret slipped around to the front to find the doors locked and barred. Hanging from the latch was a little sign, *Out To Lunch*.

Jennie Margaret frowned. "*I've* had lunch," she announced to whoever might be interested. "In fact it's almost dinner time."

She walked to a side window and peered inside curiously. There, immediately before her, frosty-cold and filled to the brim, sat a squat, glistening water cooler. It was almost too much to bear; Jennie Margaret stood on tiptoe and watched a drop of water no bigger than a tear roll down the outside of the cooler.

"Oh, dear," she whispered, and tore herself from the window to explore the back door. To her joy it was unlocked. She seized the knob and turned it.

"Oh!" she cried, startled. "Oh, I thought you were out to lunch!"

The young man who stepped outside to confront her managed also to block the passage. He was an exceedingly well-groomed young man. Smiling politely at him, Jennie Margaret was nevertheless aware of the knifelike crease in his trousers, the gleaming whiteness of his collar and the trim, flaming silk tie. And his face was alarmingly tidy and smooth; the flesh was stretched taut across its bones as though pinned tightly behind his ears, and his

41

nose had been broken several times until it was but a suggestion of a nose. A tiny smile hovered across his mouth, never allowing it to relax. Except for the twitching lips the face was as immobile and blank an an egg shell. Jennie Margaret shivered.

"I . . . I just want a drink," she explained.

The young man said nothing but his lip curled ironically. Jennie Margaret sighed and walked impatiently around him. "I'll just be a minute," she added.

But he, too, moved, and in such a manner as to prevent her from entering the garage. "We've got no water," he announced flatly.

Jennie Margaret frowned. It was quite possible they misunderstood one another; with great kindness and tact she repeated, "No water? Did you say *no water* in the cooler by the window?"

"That's it," said the young man clearly. "No water. The cooler's empty. Sorry."

"Oh, but it isn't, it isn't!" cried Jennie Margaret, and then because it was so absurd to be arguing with him she smiled and this time ducked beneath his elbow.

She had misjudged the young man. He moved as swiftly as a cat. "Get out of here," he snarled. "Get out of here, understand?"

"You're hurting me!" gasped Jennie Margaret. "My arm! Oh, please let go my arm!"

The young man smiled but his fingers tightened around her arm. Jennie Margaret closed her eyes with the pain of it.

"Maybe you didn't hear me. I said get out."

Jennie Margaret nodded. Her arm was suddenly released and they stared at one another wordlessly. Then she fled.

The bruise on her arm was swelling; Jennie Margaret examined it broodingly. She might show it to her father but on the other hand she had quite a reputation for bravery at the orphanage and enjoyed herself thoroughly in the role of martyr. She sat down on the bunk and arranged her sleeve so that her wound did not show.

"But I'm still thirsty," she sighed, "and I just don't understand about that dreadful young man."

Hearing voices she leaned forward and saw that Jeremy had returned and had encountered her foe. In an instant Jennie Margaret had forgotten her bruise.

"I want Mr. Petrie," Jeremy was saying. "I owe him five dollars for a new muffler."

"No kidding?" mocked the young man.

"Well, now, and who are you?" demanded Jeremy.

"Don't get excited, and the name's Smiley. You live here?"

Jeremy shook his head patiently. "No, I don't," he said, "and if you'll just call Mr. Petrie I'll be off on my travels."

The nervous, ugly smile deepened; Smiley was grinning. "No need to call Petrie, no need at all. That your buggy?"

He walked across the yard toward the Caravan, pulling Jeremy with him, not rudely but gently as though willing to condescend to any kindness to pry him from the door.

"I just want to pay my five dollars and leave," said Jeremy stubbornly.

"Give me the five dollars. I'll pay him."

"No," said Jeremy firmly, "no, I won't. I don't trust your friend Mr. Petrie and it was clear he didn't trust me. I'll pay nobody but him."

"I'm his nephew," Smiley said suddenly. "He'll be back in an hour, maybe two, maybe three." His mouth curved as though smiling at a secret joke. "Maybe not 'til tomorrow. Still care to wait?"

Jeremy shrugged and handed him the money. "There was something about parking, too," he confessed, not wishing to be dishonest.

Smiley held up an immaculate hand. "Forget it," he said. "You heard me, forget it."

Jeremy hesitated.

"I said forget it, and get your buggy out of here."

Jennie Margaret moved timidly from the window, lest Jeremy know that she had seen him dealt with so roughly. But when Jeremy climbed into the Caravan she was surprised to see that he was chuckling.

"That Petrie fellow will sure be mad," he said as much to himself as to her. "He got his five dollars but he didn't get his parking fee. No, sir, not from me."

It was the source of deep satisfaction.

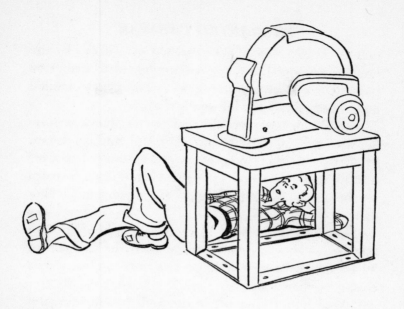

THE driver's seat of the Caravan had long ago been a
leather desk chair, but in Jeremy's hands several inches of
leg had been removed and an extra cushion added so that
what it lacked now in smartness was more than compensated for by comfort. The little seat beside it was much
newer and had chromium curves shaped like neon tubes
but the padding was thin and there were no arms. Over
the windshield, suspended from a crimson cord, hung a
plastic dog, a rabbit's foot, and a miniature hula girl.
These were Jeremy's good luck tokens.

Jeremy climbed into the driver's seat of the bus and
started the motor expectantly. The engine purred, as
well-behaved as any bus in the state of Vermont, and with
a tight feeling of regret Jeremy shifted gears. The new

quietness saddened him for he had grown to like the raucous noise of the unmuffled engine; with a sigh he pushed back the emergency brake and the Caravan rolled majestically down the hill southward.

Behind him Jeremy could hear Jennie Margaret moving about, banging pots and pans and rattling dishes. Presently the savory odor of frying hamburgers met his nostrils and he sniffed appreciatively; his enthusiasm mounted as he thought he detected the pungent smell of onions.

"They taught her right," Jeremy said to himself. "Not that I ever believed woman's place was in the kitchen, but 'til they teach men how to cook it's real nice having a cookin' woman about."

Behind him a floor board creaked. Jennie Margaret was suddenly at his elbow, her underlip thrust out belligerently.

"Father," she said angrily, "Father, there's a boy in back."

Jeremy said stupidly, "A *what?*"

"A boy," she repeated impatiently. "A boy. He's fast asleep in the machine shop in back."

"No, I'm not," protested a strange voice behind Jeremy. "I'm not a boy and I'm not asleep."

With a startled grunt Jeremy reached for the brake; the Caravan skidded to a halt. "What in tarnation goes on here?" he asked grimly. "Who are you, and how in thunder did you get into my Caravan?"

The boy might have been fifteen or he might have been

twenty; he had that adolescent look of all bone and no flesh, with the Adam's apple pushing from his throat when he talked, but the line of his jaw was firm and clean-cut and he held his head high. His clothes, although nearly threadbare, were scrupulously clean. On the whole Jeremy was more startled than alarmed.

"I climbed in while you were gone," said the boy. "I'm running away." His eyes spoke to Jeremy urgently through a screen of pride. "I've got ten dollars. I want to go south—anywhere. Could you give me a ride?"

"What you running away from?" asked Jeremy sharply.

The boy jerked his head toward Jennie Margaret; he pointed at the emblem still sewed to her sleeve. "I don't belong to anyone," he said. "I grew up same place as she did."

Jennie Margaret said softly, "I didn't see you there. I don't know you."

"Of course not. Mr. Petrie hired me out when I was twelve. I'm seventeen now," he added proudly.

"Petrie!" grunted Jeremy. "Where is that Petrie, any-way? I been lookin' for him. Owed him money but he was out."

The boy's face paled, a kind of nameless fear spilling from his eyes, but he said nothing.

"You didn't answer my question," said Jeremy. "What you running away from?"

"He beat me," was the boy's low reply.

"Beat you!" Jeremy snapped irritably. "What right

have I got to believe you? There's a law against kidnapping, you know."

"I'm seventeen," the boy replied quietly. "I'm almost grown up."

Jennie Margaret tugged at her father's sleeve gently. He became aware of many horns blowing to the rear, of people shouting. He saw that he had stopped the Caravan at an intersection and was blocking the road; it did not improve his temper.

"All right, all right," Jeremy shouted. The red flush spread to the back of his neck as he backed the Caravan from the road.

"I have to go back and turn the hamburgers," said Jennie Margaret wistfully. "We're going to have such a nice dinner." She smiled timidly at the boy as she left.

"I just want to hitch a ride," begged the boy. "I want to get out of Gallup Corners. I haven't done anything."

"Who said you had?"

"And like I said, I got a little money. Honest, sir."

"What's your name?"

"Reuben Malone."

"And he beat you. You're telling the truth?"

For a moment Jeremy thought the boy hesitated. Then he straightened. "Yes," he replied simply.

He's like me, thought Jeremy; he's like I was at that age, only he's learning how to carry himself; they grow up faster now. There's not much else to say for him, he's thin, with too few meals under his belt but at least he doesn't look as if he'd stick a knife in my back and run off with my money.

Aloud he said, "All right, Reuben, you've hitched yourself a ride to Philadelphy. Jennie Margaret," he shouted, "lay another place at the table. Hungry, Reuben?"

Reuben's eyes shone, "Yes, sir. Oh, yes, sir."

Jeremy chuckled hollowly. "Pretty near starved, myself. We'll park down the river and eat."

As the motor purred into life again Jeremy reflected, not without amusement, that for a man who had started the day alone he was finishing it in style.

Eight o'clock dinner in the Caravan was an event; the fare was plain but each of them ate with relish after their emotional trials of the day. Jeremy was the only one with something on his mind; he was considering his budget, the prospect of adding ten dollars to it, and the question of Reuben's truly owning such a sum.

But when they had finished their meal, Jeremy's newest guest removed the money from his pocket and laid it on the table. "I'd better give it to you now," Reuben said. "I hope it's enough."

"You're a good boy," Jeremy said, brightening. "I could say 'Keep it', real heartylike, but I'm a poor man with the future not as pink as it might be. I'll take your money, Reuben, with many thanks for it, too, but if it doesn't cost ten dollars to feed you then you'll have the rest of it back in Philadelphy." He pocketed the money with satisfaction.

"If I had ten dollars," said Jennie Margaret wistfully, "I'd give it to you, too, Father."

"I hope you'd be more sensible," twinkled Jeremy. "Now see here, Reuben, what do you say to writing Mr. Petrie a word or two about you tonight? I got writing paper and stamps right here. No man is all bad; he may have taken to worrying about you."

It was clear that Mr. Petrie had encouraged Reuben to be seen rather than heard; upon hearing himself addressed, Reuben sat forward on the edge of his chair, cleared his throat and frowned. His face was pale in the lamplight; a lock of stiff, sandy hair hung over one eye. He said cautiously, "Mr. Peel, I'll write him, honest I will. Only couldn't I do it later?"

"Reuben is a hero, Father, I wish you wouldn't nag at him." Jennie Margaret tilted her chin defiantly at Jeremy and turned back to Reuben. "Did it hurt terribly much to be beaten? Once I sprained my ankle; do you think it hurt as much as that?"

Reuben smiled; his frown disappeared and the corners of his eyes crinkled pleasantly. "I'm sure it couldn't have hurt as much as your sprained ankle," he said gently, and Jennie Margaret's heart was completely won.

"I'm going to be a trapeze artist when I grow up," she confided. "Did you know my mother was a star in the circus and my father used to be a clown?"

Reuben whistled faintly. "No kidding!"

"Whoa now," cried Jeremy. "You're too much the press agent for me." He said to Reuben, "I'll show you a woman who was the finest performer in the world; if Jennie Margaret grows up to be half as pretty as her, she'll make me very, very proud."

They watched as Jeremy unpinned and brought to them the picture of Madeline De Perchon in her pink silk tights.

"Oh, I don't think she's so pretty," Reuben announced. "Not as pretty as those other girls over there."

"Maybe not," said Jeremy firmly, "but those others are just movie actresses. I *knew* this woman." He added shyly, "She's Jennie Margaret's mother."

This indeed threw a different light upon the photograph, and Reuben examined it with more interest and an eye for detail.

"I think she was the most beautiful woman ever born," Jennie Margaret declared, looking over Reuben's shoulder. Jeremy nodded, for he believed this, too, and with a last wistful glance at the picture he returned it to its niche before it could be soiled or creased.

"I shall be a big league baseball player when I'm grown up," Reuben volunteered suddenly. "A pitcher, I think."

"Can you pitch?" asked Jeremy kindly.

Reuben flushed. "Not very well. But they'll teach me, you wait and see. They have farm teams and stuff like that. Someday you'll be wanting my autograph on a baseball; I'll be famous and rich, that's what I'll be."

Jennie Margaret's eyes admired him silently. "If you're going to be that famous," she said, "I'm not going to wait. Will you autograph my new red ball tomorrow? It's not a baseball but it bounces, really it does."

Reuben agreed to do this for Jennie Margaret.

"Now see here," Jeremy said with a glance at the clock. "I don't know what time youngsters go to bed these days, but it's nine-thirty and *my* bedtime's ten o'clock. I think you'd better git."

"Where's Reuben going to sleep?"

"Don't worry about me," put in Reuben swiftly. "I can just sleep in a chair."

"Well now, boy, I'm not worrying about you at all, but I might have if I hadn't got me an idea awhile back. I've thought of just the place for you. The luggage rack."

"Luggage rack?" echoed Reuben and Jennie Margaret.

"Yes, sir, the luggage rack. It's no more than a fence around the roof of the Caravan but it's good and strong; figured on taking it off when I bought the Caravan but the darn thing wouldn't come off."

"It sounds good to me," Reuben cried, flushing. "It's mighty kind of you, Mr. Peel."

"Put some color in your cheeks, too," Jeremy muttered. Once again he was struck by the resemblance between himself and Reuben, for Jeremy, released from emotions much larger than himself by his newly captured freedom, akin to the gods by his recent independence, had of late discovered within himself, as if these gifts were not enough, a rather humble but exhilarating wisdom. A poor, discouraged fellow I was at that age; life seemed very bleak, he thought objectively. And for a moment Jeremy questioned the advisability of ever being young.

They made Jennie Margaret a bed on the trunk and then went out under the stars to arrange Reuben comfortably for the night.

"Don't think it'll rain before morning, do you, Reuben?"

"No, sir, I'm sure it won't. And Mr. Peel, I thank you for taking me with you."

"Shucks," grimaced Jeremy. "Here, give me a hand to the roof, will you, boy?"

The night was soft and dark, the sky peppered with silver; a crescent moon cradled itself in the top of the trees. It was good to be out of doors, and for a moment Jeremy made only a pretense at arranging the coverlets.

"There's the Big Dipper," he observed, "and darned if that isn't the Milky Way over there. You just stop a minute, Reuben, and think of all the people under those stars; makes the chills come over me to think how big the world is. But I'll bet you, Reuben, we're the only folks lookin' at those stars this minute. Folks don't look at stars any more, not folks like us with food in our stomachs. No, sir, people keep their noses pointed at their feet nowadays, and if anybody steps on their toes they get fightin' mad, boy. It's a selfish world, take it from me. A funny world."

"You can say that again," Reuben said drowsily.

"I'd like to," Jeremy remarked grimly. "Well, good night there, Reuben, sleep well."

"Good night, Mr. Peel."

Jeremy left the boy curled up in his blankets, not quite asleep, his face shining faintly under the moon.

It's been a long day, thought Jeremy as he jumped from the roof and went into the Caravan.

IN the morning the Caravan crossed the Vermont state
line to enter Massachusetts. It was a lovely trip through
the Berkshires, over rushing mountain brooks tossed
silver by their tumultuous descent, and everywhere the
soft green of hilltops swept clean by the shadows of
passing clouds. But Nemesis, the goddess of vengeance,
waited patiently for them.

They had stopped several times that morning, Jennie
Margaret to buy groceries that Reuben carried stoically
for her, or ice cream which they all consumed with

pleasure. Jeremy himself occasionally halted the **Caravan** to sharpen lawn mowers and knives at the various farmhouses they passed, stops which were to him an even greater pleasure since they to some extent made up for the pennies Jennie Margaret spent.

Now, as they drove toward Pittsfield, Jennie Margaret appointed herself lookout for such opportune side trips. She lay sprawled across the work bench in the shop, shouting her thoughts to Reuben and Jeremy at the top of her voice, and a little sulky that no one answered her. She had counted five out-of-state license plates when she spied The Car.

It was a large, old-fashioned touring car that had hugged their path for several miles. Jennie Margaret began watching it now with a proprietary interest for it was the biggest, loveliest she had ever seen. She was about to describe it ecstatically to Jeremy when the car suddenly began to wander dizzily from the left side of the road to the right side of the road, like a huge, sluggish caterpillar.

Jennie Margaret sat up stiffly. The car's unpredictable course worried her. She tried waving at the driver. Idly the car drifted toward a stone culvert and in a frenzy Jennie Margaret cried, "Stop! Stop!"

It was a moment of vast misunderstanding. Jeremy, hearing her shout, braked savagely; the bus stopped with a scream. But the touring car, swerving giddily away from the culvert, moved relentlessly toward them. With a stuttering crash Miss Anable Lea's automobile nudged its way into the rear of Jeremy Peel's Caravan.

Jennie Margaret flung herself into Jeremy's arms. "Itsmyfaultitsmyfaultitsmyfault," she sobbed.

Jeremy thrust her aside, his face stern and white as he leaped to the road. It needed but one glance from him to see that his knife-sharpening shop was hopelessly demolished. The fine machines were crushed into piles of junk, the equipment wrecked and scattered as though a giant had powdered them into nothingness with but one stroke of his hand.

This knowledge Jeremy tucked away for future mourning as he turned all of his attention to the shattered touring car. Together he and Reuben battered open the doors and lifted out a stunned but intact Miss Anable Lea.

It was apparent almost immediately that Miss Lea was a very beautiful young woman. Silver-blonde hair poured in disarray over her shoulders; the slope of her face from cheekbone to chin was breathtaking; her mouth was rich and full, the nose structurally perfect, and her eyes as she opened them a unique shade of blue.

"A princess!" whispered Jennie Margaret. "A real, live, fairy-tale princess!"

"Where the heck," murmured Miss Lea, "am I?"

Jeremy told her exactly where she was and Miss Lea nodded her head gravely as though it were the most natural thing in the world to find herself in such a predicament. Jeremy laid her gently on the grass.

"I suppose I fell asleep," she sighed. "It was most

thoughtless of me but I drove all night. I should have
known I couldn't make New York in five hours. Who's
the little girl with the eyelashes?"

"I'm Jennie Margaret."

"Well, I'm Anable Lea. Or was." Miss Lea suddenly
caught sight of her car and gave a little scream. "No,
no," she said, rising prettily to her feet. "That can't be
my car!"

"It is," Reuben said, torn between admiration for
Miss Lea and fury at such an injustice to his benefactor.
"Your car wrecked our—I mean wrecked Mr. Peel's
Caravan."

Miss Lea stared at him blankly. They were alarmed
at seeing tears in her eyes.

"Here, here," cautioned Jeremy, "you mustn't cry.
I'm sure it can be repaired."

"But I'm not thinking of that," said Miss Lea surpris-
ingly. "It isn't my car, anyway, it's Geoffrey's. I'm looking at what it's done to your bus. It *is* your bus, isn't
it, not borrowed, like mine? Because it was all my fault
and you must be thinking I'll pay for the damage but I
can't, I've only got fifteen dollars to my name. Fifteen!"
And Miss Lea burst into an hysterical laugh. "I guess
it's funny, isn't it?" But Miss Lea stopped laughing because even she could see that it was not.

Jeremy sat heavily on the grass that Miss Lea had
vacated. His legs felt numb and rubbery; his head ached.
Jennie Margaret went to him and put her arms around
his neck.

"Please," she said. "Please, I'm sure it will be all right.

I can go back to the orphanage, truly I can. And Reuben can hitch-hike to Philadelphy, can't you, Reuben? Then you'll have the money to repair the Caravan."

Jeremy shook his head dismally. "Not that much," he said.

Miss Lea frowned at the tableau and, having tucked her long hair into a knot, she succeeded in looking quite severe. Since no one paid any attention to her she strolled toward the front of the Caravan and disappeared.

"How much will it cost to have the bus fixed?" asked Reuben, rubbing his chin angrily.

"It's not the Caravan," explained Jeremy. "It's the machines. Won't be any good to me, the bus, without the equipment. The machines are expensive."

"Oh, Father," whispered Jennie Margaret.

At this moment Miss Lea reappeared, carrying a bottle of ginger ale and a small tray of peanut butter sandwiches. "I looked inside," she said pleasantly, "I hope you don't mind. I think we all need something to munch on, don't you? I'll go back for drinking glasses."

No one replied, but Jennie Margaret shot her a worshipful glance. When she returned they were all eating, if somewhat despondently. Miss Lea sat down and joined them.

"Now look here," she said firmly, "I know what you're all thinking, but you mustn't condemn me. It isn't my fault that I fell asleep at the wheel—not entirely, that is. And besides," with a stern glance at Jeremy, "I have something to say to you."

Jeremy regarded her blankly.

"I can help you," said Miss Lea, looking him squarely in the eye. "As I said before, my name is Anable Lea. I'm twenty-three, I am in good health and," modestly, "men are always falling in love with me. But what is most important is the fact that I am a press agent."

She swallowed the last of her peanut butter sandwich and went on in a clear, forceful voice. "Until yesterday I had a job but, unfortunately, life being what it is, today I have no job and what's more I'm very, very broke. It seems to me that we might all of us get together and make the most of this impossible situation."

They stared at her, Jeremy with surprise, Jennie Margaret with unconcealed admiration, and Reuben with polite interest.

"What I mean is this," resumed Miss Lea, polishing off her sandwich with a blade of grass. "You have a Caravan here that's cute; it has possibilities. I heard what Mr. Peel said about his financial problem and it has occurred to me that among the four of us we might hit on something new for the Caravan. Knife-sharpening seems at best an unremunerative business. Why not," asked Miss Lea reasonably, "make pots of money?"

They nodded, hypnotized.

"What's more," said Miss Lea innocently, "I'm not averse to making a little money myself. I'd stick with you."

"But can you be trusted?" hazarded Reuben.

Miss Lea appeared properly shocked; it was obvious this had not occurred to her. "How can you say a thing like that?" she demanded. "I'm trying to help you!"

"Come now, Reuben," said Jeremy mildly. "Miss Lea has an idea and I haven't. I thank you, Miss Lea, you mean well, I'm sure, but I'm afraid I'm out of business."

"That's impossible," Miss Lea announced firmly. "There is no such thing as defeat."

"What's a press agent?" asked Jennie Margaret, who had been examining the word in her mind.

Miss Lea threw up her hands. "What isn't a press agent!" she replied. "Ever since Cinderella's pumpkins were turned into coaches and her rags into satin, people have been demanding fairy godmothers. That's what a press agent is, Jennie Margaret: I help make stars out of people no one has ever heard of; I think of ways to make successful people stay on top of the ladder." She sighed. "Right now my silver wand seems a little rusty."

"Father used to be a clown," said Jennie Margaret.

Miss Lea considered this, her brows puckered.

"Could we give shows?" pleaded Jennie Margaret. "I could be a trapeze artist. I could begin practicing right now."

"Not practical," murmured Miss Lea absently. "No, it will have to be something to sell to people."

"But I don't have any money to stock the Caravan; I'm not even sure I can pay for repairs," protested Jeremy.

"Money," groaned Miss Lea. "Well, it's something we shall need and we must face it. Tell me, are you willing to incorporate your Caravan, Mr. Peel?"

"Well—yes," replied Jeremy.

"Oh, what fun!" cried Jennie Margaret.

Miss Lea's glance rested questioningly upon Reuben.

"I'm just along for the ride," Reuben said sadly. "I don't belong here, you see."

"Oh, no, Reuben," cried Jennie Margaret. "No, **no,** Miss Lea, he's with us. Isn't he, Father?"

Jeremy smiled. "Reuben may not want to belong **with us.** He may be in a hurry to get to Philadelphy."

"I'm in no hurry," Reuben said breathlessly.

"Then you're with us!"

Reuben was one of them, but it was apparent that no one held any hopes for their future. His throat thick with a sigh, Jeremy attempted in some fashion to bring back the happiness of only a few moments ago. He reminded himself that he was still whole and of sturdy heart, that Pittsfield might have boiler rooms waiting just for him and that later there might be another Caravan, another chance. But it was an argument without hope, and he knew it. He was fifty years old now, and tired of insecurity; the weight of it still filled his dreams at night. Miss Lea had pluck and integrity to offer herself as a sacrificial goat but he shook his head at the idea of her rescuing him. The Caravan was finished.

"If you *really* had a silver wand," said Jennie Margaret thoughtfully, "I should think you'd want to turn Father into a clown again. He must have been an awfully good clown and didn't you notice all the big signs plastered on every barn for the last five miles?"

Miss Lea jumped to her feet. "Of course, Jennie Margaret, of course! Why didn't I think of it myself?"

"Think of what?" queried Rueben and Jeremy at once.

"Why, the circus is coming to Pittsfield. Mr. Peel, you will indeed be a clown once more." She hugged Jennie Margaret gratefully.

"But that's Farnum and Zailey!" protested Jeremy. "I can't just walk in and get a job with them. They're big, they're important!"

Miss Lea laughed joyously. "But I'm a press agent," she reminded him. "I'm a wonderful press agent. Don't you worry about a thing, Mr. Peel. When I finish talking with Mr. Farnum and Mr. Zailey they'll be after you with tears in their eyes!"

Jennie Margaret relaxed; she and Father and the Caravan were not to be parted after all.

The fact that no one quite believed Miss Lea's statement that Jeremy was to become a clown with Farnum and Zailey only proved that none of them knew Miss Lea. If they had moved in different circles they might even have heard of Miss Lea, who was sometimes referred to, when other synonyms grew pallid, as a phenomenon. Anable was an extremely resourceful young woman.

As a baby, Anable had disdained the normal habits of other children and had neither cried nor blown bubbles. At six she read *Alice in Wonderland* and thought Alice very unintelligent and rather silly. At ten, believing herself too sheltered from the realities of life she ran away from home but she traveled only as far as the baggage room of the railroad station where her harassed parents found her learning to play poker with the baggage agents, and it was a prophetic commentary that Anable was the only winning member of the party, having drawn three royal flushes in a row.

When she was sixteen and refused the finishing-school background arranged for her, her parents quite logically threw in the sponge. Agreeing that she had to go somewhere and do something Anable hit upon the solution of art school. She had only a minor talent for drawing but this proved a fortunate choice for it led to the discovery of her prowess as a promoter; she became the natural leader of the more radical elements in the school, arranging exhibits and pressing affluent strangers into purchases they could not help but later regret.

Anable's first victory as a press agent occurred in New York where she alternately browbeat and charmed Pasquale de Sforza, the greatest producer on Broadway, into subsidizing a bankrupt puppet company that met in a stable. The fact that the puppeteers became the hit of the season did not surprise Anable but rather bored her for it left her with nothing to do but arrange even vaster successes.

Later, much later, she met Geoffrey Planet and this did not bore her at all because for the first time in her life she fell in love. Incredibly enough, Geoffrey was just as forceful as Anable but since he was born with a small amount of wealth and liked hunting, fishing and riding, he preferred to pour all his energies into a Vermont law practice. To Anable, Vermont did not exist; her country was bounded by the East and Hudson rivers. Nothing that she organized, and Anable put all of her creative genius into her plots, would tempt Geoffrey to become press agent material. Geoffrey was her Waterloo, and when it became apparent that surrender was Anable's only alternative—and surrender on Anable's part was unthinkable—she packed her bags, placed them in Geoffrey's automobile and made a hasty retreat from Vermont. Her impatience sent her plummeting into the lives of Jeremy, Reuben and Jennie Margaret.

Now she was prepared to wage battle for them.

THE afternoon substantiated Anable's powers as marshal. Without a word of sympathy she divested Jeremy of all his cash, counted it at a glance and told him firmly, "This makes exactly twenty-two dollars to see us through. It means we shall have to run bills, lots of bills—at the garage, at the photographers and the printing office. Shall we go?"

They left, leaving Reuben to supervise the Caravan's removal to a garage.

"Your daughter is charming," said Anable, smiling at Jennie Margaret. "Is the boy yours, too?"

"Oh my, no," Jeremy said hastily. "His name is Malone. He's a kind of addition—like you."

Anable's left eyebrow raised in spite of itself; it was possibly the first time she had ever been described as an addition.

Jeremy said shyly, "I've been wondering why you bother with us. I don't believe in prying, but it strikes me that there's people waiting for you in New York; friends of yours, maybe."

Anable smiled. "Mr. Peel," she replied, "there is honor even among thieves. If I had been tolerably well-heeled when I banged up your Caravan you would never have seen me again. As it is, I have time rather than money to squander, so let us say no more about it."

Jeremy said no more; Anable pleased him but he was too shrewd to be overwhelmed. He liked to take his time in judging people.

Once in town, Anable steered them first to a costumers, where she rented a very elegant clown suit for Jeremy and paid cash for it. Next she guided them to the printer's, and it was here that Jeremy began to suspect Anable's penchant for getting her own way.

"I would like," said Anable Lea to the young man, who looked like a rugged Union member, "some handbills and cards made up immediately."

"I'm afraid it can't be immediately," smiled the young man. "Our orders take a week. We're very rushed now."

Miss Lea glanced at him with distaste. "I don't like

to hear that," she said. "The President of the Chamber of Commerce recommended you to us especially, and I shall have to complain to him if the service is not what was promised us. In fact," said Miss Lea, looking downright icy, "I shall have to raise one whirlpool of a row."

"What is it you wanted done?" asked the man cautiously.

Anable brought out a sheet of paper with several sketches upon it. "A dozen of each."

"Well," said this ink-stained member of the proletariat, "we might have them done for you in the morning. For a small compensation, that is."

"Compensation?" Anable glanced suspiciously at him.

The man leaned forward and murmured into Anable's ear; Jeremy thought she seemed amused.

"All right," she said. "You win."

The man chuckled. "Charlie," he shouted. "Charlie, get these rolling right away. On the double."

Jeremy and Jennie Margaret were intrigued. Jeremy allowed Anable to take his arm, but when they reached the street he stopped. "We're all in this together," he said. "We're partners, you and I. I want to know what this was all about."

Anable laughed richly. "He said," she told Jeremy, "that since I knew the President of the Chamber of Commerce so well, he would insist upon my having dinner with him tomorrow night. You see, *he's* the President of the Chamber of Commerce."

"Offhand," remarked Jeremy grimly, "I'd say you

were a very reckless, ill-advised young lady. In fact, I
wonder if you're a lady at all."

"Oh, Father!" whispered Jennie Margaret, shocked.

But Anable squeezed his arm affectionately. "Mr.
Peel," she said, "I think you and I are going to get along
capitally."

At the photographers', Jeremy donned the elegant
clown suit, the large shoes and the silly hat. There was a
little mirror in the cubicle to which he had been assigned
and as each piece of his costume was added he turned
to look. It was not much like the old dressing room at
his circus, with the lights beating on his painted face,
the wisps of false hair lying about, the smell of greasepaint and the sweet memories of Madeline De Perchon,
but it brought them back vividly, excitingly, so that he
emerged from the dressing room an exalted man.

"You're the loveliest clown I've ever seen," sighed
Jennie Margaret ecstatically.

"Excellent indeed," cried the photographer with a bad
French accent and a happy glance at Anable.

"Hold still," Anable said, and painted a vast mouth on
Jeremy with her lipstick. She powdered him skillfully
from her compact and, when she had finished, the photographer took pictures of Jeremy somersaulting, of
Jeremy cavorting and cartwheeling, of Jeremy looking
monstrously sad.

"You're all right," said Anable, and meant it. She
meant, too, that Jeremy's clowning was good enough for
both of their worlds and the dignity she had glimpsed
in Jeremy was in his work, also.

"If you don't mind," she told Jeremy, "while our little chum here is finishing up and while you're getting back into your regular clothes, I have one more errand to do. If you don't mind, Mr. Peel?"

"But Jennie Margaret and I will go with you," said Jeremy. "I won't take a minute to change."

"I'd rather you didn't," Anable replied firmly. "I'd rather you didn't, really. It's just a telephone call. Jennie Margaret can wait for you."

"Telephone call? You have friends here?"

Anable looked impatient. "I'll tell you all about it later, Mr. Peel."

Recalling her bizarre tactics with the printer, Jeremy was inclined to feel uneasy about her insistence. "No," he said firmly, "No, I'll go with you, Anable."

Anable glanced at his clown costume, at the thin mask of makeup and his great flapping shoes. "You can scarcely follow me in that," she said mischievously. "I'll tell you this, Mr. Peel, it's just a long-distance call to New York. Don't you trust me? I'll make it collect, too," she added brightly, and before Jeremy could protest she had vanished.

Early the next morning Jennie Margaret stirred in her bed on the trunk and opened one eye experimentally. There was something on her mind, something big and monumental. Carefully she tested her thoughts; was it a good thing or was it bad? Was it exciting or dull? Remembering, she sat up straight.

Yes, there she was, the princess, lying in her father's

bunk across the bus. As though it were not enough to have a real father and Reuben Malone, who was a hero, there was Miss Anable Lea. Jennie Margaret wished only that Lucy might be with her to share such excitement.

"Miss Lea," whispered Jennie Margaret.

Anable opened her eyes immediately with the attitude of one to whom each new day is interesting.

"Hello, Jennie Margaret," she said. "Let's get up before those darn garage mechanics start nosing around."

With an economy of movement Anable swung herself out of the bunk and brushed her teeth at the sink. The Caravan that morning leaned heavily on jacks beside a garage called the Blue Star Station; there was not much to be seen from the windows beyond a brick wall and the side of the garage, but looking up Jennie could see blue sky and a haze of faraway mountains; by going forward to the driver's seat she could see a street where people walked and cars passed slowly by. It was a dark, narrow corner in which the Caravan had been placed and Jennie Margaret could not help sighing as she remembered their previous morning.

When they had dressed, and the coffee was bubbling on the stove, Jennie Margaret awakened Jeremy and Reuben Malone on the roof. It was a curious group that sat down to breakfast.

"Will anything nice happen today?" asked Jennie Margaret.

"Why, sure, Jennie Margaret," said Reuben, with

71

more vivacity than he had hitherto evidenced. "Something nice is bound to happen."

He received a wink from Jeremy who had slept exceedingly well and did not yet realize what a strenuous day lay before him.

With a warm glance at them all, Anable said, "This morning I shall pick up the handbills, the cards and the photographs. This afternoon Mr. Peel and I might go to the circus grounds."

"Oh, dear," Jeremy said nervously.

"And, Reuben," she continued, "I'd like you to have the garage man look over my car and put a price on it. We're going to sell it."

"Sell it!" protested Jeremy. "But it's not yours! You said so."

"Nonsense," replied Anable with dignity. "I was driving it, wasn't I? Anyway, we are going to make pots of money; I shall be able to buy Geoffrey ten cars. Sell the car, Reuben."

At noon Anable returned with the handbills and spread them out on the table. They were handsome, colorful affairs for the President of the Chamber of Commerce, whose name was Willie Rumple, had handled them himself. But they puzzled Jeremy.

"The Great Polish National Circus (they read) *presents Jeremy Peel, The Funniest Man on Earth, Warsaw Stadium, 1935. Appearing with him, The Flying Trapenzas, Critique the Sword Swallower, The Aquenda Acrobats."*

"Polish National Circus!" exclaimed Jeremy.

Anable shrugged. "You could easily have been born in Poland, couldn't you? I've made you a reputation on paper. What more could you want? Now look at the photographs; didn't they come out well?"

They studied the pictures happily; no one could criticize them, they were wonderful. Besides being glossy and satin-smooth to the touch, they presented Jeremy with an aura of importance.

"I've also brought you a drooping bow-tie," Anable said. "There was a hurdy-gurdy man on the street and he sold it to me for a quarter. It will give you just the right touch, a Continental air, you see."

She held out a long, ribbonlike blue string, faintly polka-dotted, and when Jeremy tried it on and saw that it did give him a Continental appearance he shook his head in bewilderment. If he could have met Anable's parents at that moment he would have wrung their hands in sympathy.

"I think this is it," said Anable, tugging gently at Jeremy's sleeve. "This is the third coach we've passed."

Jeremy wrenched his gaze from the panorama of circus life spread out before him. From the slope of the hill where they stood he could see smoke from a dozen fires, tents veritably springing from the earth, and trailers of every color and description; the seemingly unorganized but minutely planned movements of people, elephants and horses preparing for the greatest show on earth. Jeremy wished Jennie Margaret could be there; the sight would thrill her.

Anable was a sight no less thrilling. She wore purple shoes and gloves, a purple turban about her head and a white dress with splashes of purple about the waist. The young man who answered her knock whistled faintly.

"We'd like to see the manager," Anable informed him. "We'd like to see Mr. Turgis."

The boy nodded, moved aside, and Jeremy and Anable walked in.

The gentleman they confronted seemed so twinklingly happy that Jeremy, acquainted now with Anable's technique, felt a fleeting spasm of pity for him. Mr. Turgis sat behind a large desk in the railroad car set aside for the executives of The Great Show. Behind him on the wall hung maps and charts and a group of autographed prints; he had a look of solid permanence that cowed Jeremy but to which Anable seemed indifferent. Without hesitation she moved across the room and clasped Mr. Turgis' outstretched hand in hers.

"How do you do, Mr. Turgis," she said softly, her voice striking Jeremy as unusually shy. "I don't quite know how to explain . . ."

"Sit down, sit down," boomed Mr. Turgis, taking in Anable's ensemble with a bright eye. "Take a minute to sit down. I won't bite you."

Anable laughed tremulously and sat down. "It's this way, Mr. Turgis," she began, her eyes fastened girlishly upon him, "I'm only a very young press agent and this is clearly a job too big for me to handle. I admit that ever so frankly. This gentleman here, our client, has just arrived from Europe." She paused, allowing this to sink in.

"Has just arrived from Europe," she repeated. "He was introduced to me by Pasquale de Sforza and I feel terribly privileged to introduce him to you. Only I can see that he *needs* no introduction to *you*, Mr. Turgis. Mr. Turgis, let me present to you—oh, it is such an honor—Europe's greatest clown, Jeremy Peel."

There was a rich, fruity silence. Anable released Mr. Turgis' hand gently and he sat down. He wrinkled his brow, scratched an ear, glanced at Anable and then rested his gaze upon Jeremy.

"How do you do," he said politely.

"How do you do," replied Jeremy.

Anable beamed at them both as though they were men whom she had struggled a lifetime to bring together. Then with an air of conspiracy she laid before Mr. Turgis the photographs of Jeremy.

"I brought Mr. Peel to you as quickly as possible," she said carelessly. "I knew you'd want to meet him. We came by plane, you know. Here are two of the handbills I brought along from his portfolio. You can see by the photographs what made him so great. Aren't they precious?"

Mr. Turgis stared at them desperately. "Ah, yes," he sighed at last. "I think I recognize Mr. Peel now. Of course; yes, of course. Frightful of me, but for a moment . . ."

"Naturally. It has been so long, what with the war and all. But it's a hard face to forget, isn't it, Mr. Turgis?"

Mr. Turgis agreed. He leaned back in his swivel chair and became expansive.

"Have a cigar, Mr. Peel. Now, uh, Miss . . ."

"Miss Lea."

"Ah yes; now Miss Lea, I certainly do appreciate your coming to us and I say that from the heart." He frowned slightly. "However, since we had no advance notice—that is, our stars are naturally under contract, and I couldn't offer Mr. Peel all that he deserves immediately. You understand this, Mr. Peel?"

Jeremy nodded. He had been counseled to keep his mouth shut.

"But we do just happen to have a vacancy here, and though it's nothing permanent, still I mention it because you might like to get your hand into our American way of life. Funny thing," he said, scowling, "or pardon me, I should say a fine coincidence for you, Mr. Peel; one of our clowns was called to New York this morning. Something about a catch in his contract that had to be smoothed out at once. Well," he shrugged, "can't be helped. His partner will assume his role in the act but there *is* a place for you if you'd care to fill it. We'll be here in Pittsfield two weeks; give you a chance to have a little fun and see what we're like."

Jeremy's mouth opened but only a small gurgle like the sound of a quiet fountain issued forth. Anable said swiftly, "That seems fair enough. It's quite charming of you, Mr. Turgis. Then Mr. Peel can have his vacation and you can discuss a contract later in the year."

"Ah, yes. And, uh, as to recompense," went on Mr. Turgis, "eighty-five a week?" He smiled lushly at Anable.

To Jeremy's utter surprise—he had commanded twenty dollars a week in the old days—Anable's hands fluttered scornfully. "Come now, Mr. Turgis," she admonished. "It is, in its way, insulting that you do not give Mr. Peel full billing and a life contract, but let us not play around. Mr. Peel's talents deserve at least five hundred a week."

Mr. Turgis looked crafty. "One hundred."

"Three hundred."

"One hundred and twenty-five."

"Two hundred."

They settled at a hundred and fifty a week.

"You are prepared to begin work this afternoon?" sighed Mr. Turgis, as they signed the necessary papers.

For Anable's sake Jeremy stifled an ardent and provincial "Am I!" and replied casually that he was, indeed, prepared to begin working.

"I'll go and call Harry Olsen," said Mr. Turgis mysteriously, and disappeared.

Anable stood up, smoothing out her gloves. "Well, Mr. Peel," she said happily, "it's all yours. Don't let them frighten you. You're good."

"I don't know how to thank you," groaned Jeremy, and didn't.

Anable drew on her gloves thoughtfully. "I do think

we did rather well, but I wish I'd held out for two hundred. Turgis really is in a jam with Vladimir Peski gone to New York."

"Vladimir what?" repeated Jeremy; then in horror he snapped to attention. "How do you know his name? Mr. Turgis didn't tell you, I heard every word he said!"

For a moment Anable looked like a small child who had been caught stealing apples from the orchard; then she smiled mischievously. "Well, I only suppose it was Vladimir Peski," she admitted. "I told Pasquale de Sforza to send for the best clown he could find, and Vladimir seems to be the star here."

"Pasquale!" With startling clarity Jeremy remembered her telephone call to New York. He closed his mouth with a snap.

"Good luck to you, Mr. Peel," said Anable gently, and left him to the mercies of Mr. Farnum and Mr. Zailey.

IT was a lazy morning with the sun warm and yellow as melted butter. A brisk wind from the mountains laced the clouds across the sky. Jennie Margaret, peeling potatoes in the shelter of the Caravan, stopped to examine a new cut on her thumb. She poked at it tenderly and made a face at the knife. "Clumsy thing," she muttered.

She was quite alone. Occasionally the voices of the mechanics were blown to her, their conversation torn apart by the wind, but this morning Anable was shopping at the grocery store and Jeremy preparing for his very first performance at the circus.

Remembering last night, Jennie Margaret caught her breath. Anable had sauntered in alone, her eyes brimming with laughter. "He's in," she had cried. "Jennie Margaret, your father is a clown again."

For Reuben, who did not believe in fairy tales, this was difficult news to assimilate.

"You mean they actually hired him? They believed everything you told them?"

Anable had smiled. "It is only a matter of confidence."

But Reuben was puzzled. "Where," he had asked simply, "does one find such confidence?"

But if it was confidence that Anable radiated it was contagious, for only this morning they had overheard Reuben whistling on the roof. Two days ago it had seemed the Caravan must be abandoned; now they were joined by Anable, and Jeremy was a clown. In a few minutes Anable would walk swiftly up the street, breathless as always, a dozen heads turned to watch her. "Oh, Jennie Margaret," she would cry, "you can't imagine what happened to me downtown!" She would sit beside Jennie Margaret and warmly explain what news the grocer had imparted to her, throw up her hands in horror at Jennie Margaret's cut fingers, and make a lively adventure out of peeling potatoes.

Jennie Margaret sighed rapturously; unheeded, the knife slipped to the ground. She was carrying with her today the same warmth which the movies at the orphanage contributed, but unlike play-acting or day-dreaming it would not end in a moment to jolt her rudely back to Miss Arbuckle and a world of orphans.

A fluffy white cloud scudded fitfully across the sun and for a few seconds Jennie Margaret sat in shadow. She hesitated; it could end, it might be only a dream. When one was but thirteen, although almost fourteen, it was difficult to judge.

Frightened, she glanced up to see Anable hurrying across the yard, the wind snapping at her skirts. She increased her pace when she saw Jennie Margaret, and there was nothing dreamlike about the heavy basket of groceries she thrust at Jennie Margaret.

"You can't imagine!" she gasped. "Oh, you can't imagine all that's happened to me!" She paused to catch her breath. "Just wait, Jennie Margaret, 'til you hear what the grocer told me this morning. He said . . ."

Jennie Margaret leaned back and smiled. Everything was fine, after all. Anable did love her and Reuben *had* whistled this morning. And Father was the most wonderful clown in the world. It was real.

In the vast comings and goings of the big top, Jeremy's performance did not go unnoticed for he proved himself plucky and laughable. There was a night when, upon leaving the arena, the band of waiting bareback riders applauded kindly; and twice Harry Olsen brought to Jeremy sweet quotations of praise. Above all there were the moments, great moments indeed, when Jeremy ceased to be a human with needs and desires of his own, and became only an instrument through which poured the craft and delicacy of his art. These were the moments that fulfilled him. They dizzied him with their vision of all life might hold if each man's dream could become reality. For these few days Jeremy floated on rosy-hued clouds.

"Each night I feel bigger," he told Harry Olsen. "It's like Christmas."

"You'll be stealing the act, old boy," said Harry. "Another month and I'll be your partner."

"But I don't have a month," Jeremy replied sadly. "Only days."

As each day fled past Jeremy grew increasingly thoughtful. It was only reasonable to suppose that when he left the circus he would be swiftly forgotten. This at first he accepted with equanimity, enjoying each day to its end, but as the second week of his contract arrived he began to throw himself into the life with an abandon which he had never given to the boiler rooms. He no longer returned to the Caravan each night but, explaining to Anable the necessity of this new development, slept in Harry Olsen's trailer. Anable understood and said nothing.

In the Caravan life went on in much the same manner as before. Jennie Margaret and Anable busied themselves in cozy, homely tasks that quite surprised Anable, who found herself wrapped continually in voluminous aprons. Reuben was almost immediately befriended by the mechanics who allowed him to putter about the wreck of the Caravan's rear. But whatever separate paths they followed during the day, when evening came the three of them made their way to the fairground. It became traditional, like the mutually pleasing habits which a family acquire without effort. These excursions were never unremunerative. There was, first of all, Jeremy, whom they never tired of watching; and there were Anable's Young Men, all of them young and clean-cut—indeed, Jeremy could not tell them apart—and eager to supply Anable with ice cream, popcorn, and candy. Anable treated each of them with disinterested courtesy and sometimes could not tell them apart, either.

It was under these pleasant conditions that Jennie Margaret gained five pounds, while Reuben began to glow rosily with his first sunburn. As for Anable, any passersby seeing her dry her hair on the steps of the Caravan one brilliant morning could not have escaped the air of satisfaction that she wore. Being both resourceful and flexible, Anable was enjoying herself.

"Does it look right?" she pleaded of Jennie Margaret. "Does it look clean? Does it shine? Be honest, Jennie Margaret, because I haven't washed it myself since—since the Depression. If I was born then," she added lamely.

"It looks beautiful," said Jennie Margaret, sitting down beside her. "I've just been writing a letter to Lucy and telling her all about you. She's going to be surprised, I betcha."

"You betcha," murmured Anable, studying her nails. "My friends would be surprised if I wrote them a letter, too."

"You mean because you're with us, in the Caravan?"

Anable laughed. "Oh, no, Jennie Margaret. They'd just be surprised at my writing a letter."

"Well, I'm sure they'd love to hear from you," Jennie Margaret said politely, "and if you'd care to write them I have some lovely blue paper with kittens on it; Angora kittens. You could borrow it. Don't you ever write to the man whose car you busted up?"

"Geoffrey?" Anable smiled wryly. "What would you suggest my saying? Dear Geoffrey, your car has been wrecked and I am selling it for one hundred dollars, love, Anable?"

"Well," said Jennie Margaret with dignity, "you could just send him your love. He's your boyfriend, isn't he?"

"Yes and no."

"Well, that doesn't make much sense."

"I don't know about you, Jennie Margaret," said Anable impatiently, "but there are some people on this earth that I just can't get along with. I fell in love with one of them."

"What happened?" asked Jennie Margaret.

"We had a fight and I walked out."

"It sounds to me," said Jennie Margaret wisely, "like those stories where the hero and the heroine love each other so much they fight all the time. I get a little tired of those stories."

"It's no wonder," Anable said moodily. "You have no idea how tiring the real thing can be."

Jennie Margaret pondered the problem of being adult. There were moments when it sounded very dismal. "Where is Geoffrey now?" she asked at length.

84

"I am quite sure he is exactly where I left him. In fact, it is doubtful whether he has moved an inch from Stonewall, Vermont, bless his brilliant soul. Hello there, Reuben."

"Hello," Reuben said, appearing suddenly around the corner. "Anable, what are we having for dinner? Is it us that smells so good?"

Anable laughed, "It isn't Casey's Grill next door; it's us all right. Jennie Margaret and I are trying a roast of beef; one more hour and it'll be in your mouth. How's the Caravan look today?"

"Oh, gosh," Reuben said, his eyes shining. "Just wait 'til Mr. Peel comes back. The repairs are going to start showing now. He'll be so proud!"

"Or wait 'til he hears Anable's plan," corrected Jennie Margaret. "That's even bigger than one new fender."

"Well," said Anable cheerfully, "I'm going in and peek at the roast. It does smell good, doesn't it?"

"Reuben," whispered Jennie Margaret when she had gone inside, "Reuben, do you know anything about love?"

Reuben was startled. "Me?" He poked his finger into his chest. "My gosh no, Jen. Why do you whisper, anyway? What's the matter with you? Are you sick?"

"Oh, for goodness sake," Jennie Margaret said, "I guess I can't talk to *you.*" She stood up and conscientiously dusted off the back of her dress. "You just go back to your dirty old work and never mind."

"Your nose is smudged," teased Reuben.

"Oh!" she cried indignantly, and left him laughing in

the doorway. She tiptoed into the Caravan and quietly, surreptitiously, removed from the bookcase her writing pad and pencil. Then, with an ear cocked for any adventuring footsteps, she sat on the steps and began a laborious note that she had romantically planned for some time. It was addressed to Stonewall, Vermont.

It was Friday night. Emerging from his dressing room Jeremy passed the Fat Lady sitting on an orange crate knitting a sweater for her daughter in Bayonne, New Jersey. The Fat Lady smiled at him.

"Almost ready to leave us, I hear."

Jeremy nodded. "Almost."

She winked at him. "You're with it," she said. "You'll get along."

Jeremy waved good night to her and passed from the circle of light into darkness. It was midnight; the fairgrounds were hushed and emptied; one last evening and the tents would quietly vanish to appear again in another state, another city. For tonight, Jeremy's sorrow at being left behind was diminished by a most compelling urge to discover what Anable planned next for the Caravan; his conception of home had shifted momentarily from Harry Olsen to Jennie Margaret, so that as he sauntered idly toward the bus stop he felt no reluctance at leaving Harry, but rather a curious excitement as to what his wages had bought for the Caravan.

As he reached the corner a pale oval disengaged itself from a nearby telegraph pole and Jeremy realized that he was not alone.

"Warm, isn't it, sir?"

There was a familiar thread to the voice that caused Jeremy to lean forward, "Why," he cried, examining the dim face, "it's Mr. Bowler, isn't it? Herb Bowler?"

The figure drew closer and the two men peered at one another in the gloom.

"Why, Mr. Peel," murmured Herb. They shook hands heartily.

"This is a surprise!"

"Isn't it? What are you doing here?"

"Well, what are *you* doing here?"

They continued to wring each others' hands. It was the profound mystery of life that they should meet again.

"I'm a clown now," confided Jeremy. "I've been hitting the big time, Herb, really hitting it. Things have been looking up since Gallup Corners, boy."

"Is that a fact?" cried Mr. Bowler.

"It's a fact, all right."

"And did you find your daughter well, Mr. Peel?"

Jeremy grinned. "She's with me, Herb. Quite a girl if I say so myself. How are the books coming along?"

Mr. Bowler's aura of good cheer dissolved. He seemed actually to shrink in size, as though he had been hit below the belt. "Not so good, Mr. Peel, not so good," he said. "I've been serving the American Public like I told you, but Mr. Peel I'm not so sure they want to be served." He shook his head sadly. "All my books, my beautiful books that I was going to sell, they don't want 'em, Mr. Peel." He put down his satchel and moved his hands helplessly. It was apparent that he was close to tears. "I got books on the Russian policy, I got books on the atom bomb and the United Nations—you and me, we know what a mess the world's in but it don't seem as though the American People want to know. All they want," he cried, "are comic books."

"Comic books?" whispered Jeremy, startled.

"Comic books! Time and again they ask for Super Smith's Snooper Books. They just don't want to know about the Balkans or the Ruhr. I'm telling you, Mr. Peel, just between you and me it's disillusioning."

"I can see that," responded Jeremy. He could also see that Herb was only a ghost of his former self. It pained him to see his old friend in such a condition.

"It's too bad, Herb," he said gravely. "But just think how Lincoln must have felt when all the people were against him. He's a hero now; maybe you'll be a hero."

"But they killed him," Herb said miserably.

Jeremy shook his head. "It's always darkest before the dawn, Herb."

"I guess you're right," he sighed.

A vegetable truck roared past them and slithered to a stop down the road; a head was pushed from its window. "Hey, you guys want a lift?"

"Sure," Jeremy shouted. Turning to Herb he said, "You take the ride, boy, I'd only be in the way. Maybe you can sell him a book."

Herb stared at him numbly so that Jeremy was forced to propel him forward. At the same time he slipped ten dollars in Mr. Bowler's shabby back pocket.

"You guys think I'm a taxi?" bellowed the truck driver.

"Here he is," said Jeremy. "You take care of him, he's a friend of mine. A good fellow."

"You the King of England or sumpin?" muttered the truck driver.

"Thanks, Mr. Peel," said Herb, brightening. "It sure was a coincidence, our meeting here, wasn't it? I'll remember what you said, Mr. Peel. Good-bye."

Jeremy watched the truck disappear down the road; then, with a sigh, he climbed wearily aboard the bus that would return him to the door of his Caravan. But his thoughts all the way home concerned Herb Bowler and the peculiar problem of the American Public.

THE Caravan stood on its four wheels with a new and glamorous, glassed-in rear. In the morning sunlight Jeremy surveyed it and felt increasingly tender toward the world.

"Yes, sir," he said, "she looks like a million dollars!"

"We're going to paint her, too," said Reuben confidentially. "That is, if it's all right with you."

Jeremy smiled. His arm rested lightly on Jennie Margaret's shoulder and felt curiously at home there.

It occurred to him that he had missed many important years of her life and this gave him a pang that was not at all in concurrence with his former reluctance to open his heart to her. "You've done a great job," he said. "Anything's all right with me. Anything."

"Then this is what we've planned," explained Anable, consulting a thin notebook and not at all ashamed of taking advantage of Jeremy's benevolent mood. "We've figured it all out. Once Reuben knew a boy who made tons of money selling ice cream and candy one summer. He had a red cart with an awning."

"And so we want to sell ice cream and candy, Father," cried Jennie Margaret. "Oh, how jealous Lucy will be!"

"Well," said Jeremy. "Well, well, well!" He removed his arm from Jennie Margaret's shoulder and turned to look at Anable. "You, too?" he asked sternly. "You've paid your debt to us, you know. You're free now, Anable."

Jennie Margaret reached out and dug her nails into Reuben's arm. She had never considered the possibility of Anable's leaving them, but all of a sudden she realized the impenetrable distance of age between herself and Anable and she knew that nothing could hold grownups if they did not want to be held. They alone were free in her world.

"Of course it means me," Anable said angrily. "My goodness," she said, "you don't think I'd leave now when you're going to make pots of money?"

A slow smile illuminated Jeremy's features. "Pots of money?" he repeated. "With ice cream and candy?"

"Mr. Peel," she replied coolly, "one successful Candy Caravan may give way to many successful Caravans. Eventually there might be a whole fleet of busses spreading over the entire country."

"And Anable's sold the car for a hundred dollars," broke in Reuben. "Everything's going to be all right, Mr. Peel."

Jeremy glanced at Reuben, at his eager brown face; at Jennie Margaret, radiant in the green uniform that Anable had cleverly made over for her; at the three of them standing close to each other in the sunshine, and Jeremy's heart quickened with pride and affection. Anable is our good luck piece, he thought suddenly. Just look at us. Of course everything is going to be all right.

Aloud he said, "Then we'd better get going, folks. Matinee starts at two-thirty sharp!"

"Matinee!" shouted Jennie Margaret. She seized Anable by the arm and hugged her. "It's Father's last day, and we'll be moving soon in our own Candy Caravan. Oh, I couldn't have stood it if you'd left us, Anable. Honest."

"Who's buying our soda pop tonight?" asked Reuben. "Willie Rumple or the funny one with the pink moustache?"

"Mr. Rumple," said Anable, smiling. "Only don't make fun of him. He's really very nice. Those garage mechanics are making you very flip, Reuben."

"Here he comes now," said Jeremy. "Where is my lunch?"

Mr. Rumple seemed agitated today. He was extremely

well-scrubbed and there was not a trace of ink about him. While they ate lunch he sat and amiably conversed with Jeremy, but his eye wandered discriminately toward Anable.

"May I see you alone sometime today?" he whispered as Anable arose to remove the dishes. "Please?"

Anable glanced at him, noticed the beads of sweat upon his brow, the humorless glaze of his eyes and knew that he planned to propose to her; somehow she resented it.

"Perhaps," she replied. "Right now I've got to dress. And then you know we're all going to the circus and then we're going to have dinner and go to the circus again. And following the evening show Mr. Olsen has invited us to his trailer for a small party."

Mr. Rumple knew, and his jaw tightened. "I'll risk it," he said humbly. "I'll be sitting on the step outside, in case you want me."

Mr. Rumple gathered his dignity about him and retreated to the steps where he sat down, taking care not to soil his trousers. He fumbled with his pipe and had just succeeded in making it draw well when a shadow fell over him, a long shadow that startled him, for he had felt himself to be alone. He looked up and found himself regarded curiously by a young man in a taffy-colored Palm Beach suit. The stranger was just under six feet tall and extremely well-built, with the heaviness that accompanies an athlete when he is attired for the street. As they examined one another Mr. Rumple's intruder suddenly smiled. "Miss Lea here?" he asked.

"Why, yes. She's inside."

Apparently the young man needed no further information. He stepped quickly to the door, leaned over Mr. Rumple and called, "Anable? Anable?"

"You know Miss Lea?"

"Naturally," replied the young man drily.

Within a moment Anable opened the door, one hand absently engrossed in securing her belt. She glanced at the young man and turned crimson.

"Geoffrey!" she faltered.

Geoffrey reached out to her but in their attempt to embrace they discovered that Mr. Rumple was in the way; that it could not be done.

"Well, come in," Anable said helplessly. "Geoffrey, it's wonderful that you came, but how in the world did you find me? Darling, come in."

She smiled warmly at Mr. Rumple but left him sitting wistfully on the steps.

"I had a case," Geoffrey explained. "It was a dandy, Anable. Went very well and when it was finished I thought *Why Not?* So I grabbed the next plane and here I am, fresh from the hinterland. You left mighty suddenly, Anable; it was depressing, I must say. Now let's talk. Let's talk the whole affair over logically and get down to a solution. I'm a reasonable man, darling, but I've got only tonight, I have to be on the midnight plane and darn it, I love you. This can't just go on and on."

"Of course not," agreed Anable. "Oh, Geoff, let me look at you. You're browner, you look splendid." She asked suspiciously, "You've been enjoying yourself?"

"I'll say," grinned Geoffrey. "I'll tell you about the case when we've settled Us. I was deucedly clever, Anable, if I say so myself. And in courting you, my sweet, I have to sing my own praises."

"Geoff, that isn't so."

"Of course it's so," he told her emphatically. "The whole battle concerns who is going to manage who."

"Whom," she corrected automatically, and then laughed. "Darling, let's forget the battles. I want you to meet . . ."

He laid a finger over her lips. "On the contrary, I have it all worked out," he said. "I've decided we're simply too strong willed, both of us. Instead of analyzing all our disagreements *I* say let's just get married and see what happens."

"Geoffrey, please," Anable pleaded.

"Please what? Darling, I tell you it's all so ridiculous. Why keep shoving me into a square box? I'm disgustingly round, you know. You can't change me."

"It isn't that at all, Geoffrey Planet," retorted Anable hotly. "I simply want a husband who—who . . ."

"You see?" Geoffrey teased. "You haven't the faintest idea of what you want. But you do want me."

Anable flushed. "I think it's incredibly bad taste arguing over this as though it were a business deal or a— a law case."

Geoffrey mockingly smote his forehead. "You women!" he growled. "You want . . ."

"Well, well, well," said Jeremy, walking into the cabin. "Thought I heard voices. Who's this, Anable? Another boyfriend of yours?"

"Yes," said Anable coolly. "Just another boyfriend, Mr. Peel."

Geoffrey laughed. "I'm delighted to meet you, sir. Don't you have a young daughter by the name of Jennie Margaret? I'm especially interested in making her acquaintance."

"Oh, I want you to," cried Anable warmly.

"Are you really Geoffrey?" asked Jennie Margaret, peering over the partition like a pixie. She walked shyly in to greet him, very gay in new hair ribbons, her face scrubbed until it shone.

"Hello," said Geoffrey.

"Hello," responded Jennie Margaret, shaking his hand.

"It's time we were off," Jeremy said politely. "I guess you'll be wanting to join us later, Anable. You just go along with your friend."

Geoffrey seemed surprised. "I'm interrupting something?"

"It doesn't matter," Anable said. "It's Mr. Peel's last day with the circus but we can just—I mean, we were going to attend not one but *two* performances," she laughed. "It's all right, Geoffrey. And I know a wonderful place where we can go."

"You're in the circus, are you?" Geoffrey asked with interest. He reached for Anable's hand and folded it into his. "Darling, I don't want to break up your **party** and I love circuses, I always did. It wouldn't be the same party if I took you away. I insist upon joining it; the show must go on."

The pressure of his hand upon Anable's was firm and endearing; Anable sighed. What Geoffrey said was perfectly true, the party would not be the same without her, but she would have preferred logic to be withdrawn. She would also have preferred a few hours alone with him, but for the moment it appeared that his mere presence would have to suffice.

"All right," she said reluctantly, "let's go."

The circus had begun its last performance. The band hurtled itself into a Sousa march, the strident voice of the cymbals cutting the air crisply at every downbeat while at another level the drums rolled out their ancient rhythms. Into the arena poured the clowns, tumbling, ludicrous, their antics a marvel of flexion. Then came the bareback riders, the ponies riding sweetly, heads down, under their burden. The sequins of the acrobats sparkled richly as all over the arena they hung from their fragile ropes, hair tossing in a symphony of movement, their smiles quick and breathless. Handsome young men with sinewy muscles swung the pretty girls on their shoulders and leaped into space. There were elephants and monkeys and lions, all with an intelligence in the ring that mocked and satirized Man's brightest hopes. The music crashed at the eardrums, pulling, emphatic; there was no end to it. It was the final product, the ultimate in theater.

"Isn't Father wonderful?" breathed Jennie Margaret. "He's terrific!"

"He's funny; funniest of them all." And the circus to each of them was a personal, intimate thing for Jeremy was a part of it.

But Anable was not enjoying the evening.

As the performance progressed, and Jeremy's roles were ended, Anable's glance turned critically, then reproachfully toward Geoffrey. At first, caught in the thrill of displaying her new friends to him, she outdid herself in enthusiasm, daring Geoffrey to find one error, one fault in Jeremy or Reuben or Jennie Margaret. When he found none, she grew angry that he enjoyed them so thoroughly. Indeed, as the hours flew past and Geoffrey addressed himself to them all, not even excluding the strangers who sat on either side, Anable saw that he was having a perfectly wonderful time. It was quite possible that Geoffrey had forgotten his mission; it was probable, or so at least thought Anable, that he had quite forgotten her.

When the performance had ended, and the vast tent began emptying itself, Anable stood up with a wicked glint in her eye.

"It's over," she said icily. "Isn't that too bad, Geoffrey?"

Geoffrey glanced at his watch. "Well," he observed, "I should say it's time it was over. My plane leaves in half an hour; I shall have to rush."

Anable, who had already consulted her watch said mockingly, "Half an hour?"

He smiled. "Darling, it's been wonderful. I feel so refreshed; you always do that to me. We have such fun together, don't we."

"Fun?" parroted Anable. "Fun, darling?"

He glanced at her quickly. "Anable, you're not angry?"

"Angry?"

Geoffrey flushed. "We can talk on the way if that's what you mean. You'll come to the airport with me? But I really enjoyed all this."

"You're just a boy at heart, aren't you?" she remarked coldly.

"Aren't we all?"

"Possibly. You also take me for granted."

Geoffrey raised his arms hopelessly. "We're adults," he said. He grasped her hand warmly, urgently. "Anable, why not fly back with me tonight to Vermont? We could be married tomorrow. Will you?"

"No."

"Why not?"

"Because I'm busy."

"And may I ask busy with what? With whom?"

"You wouldn't understand," she replied with a thread of seriousness in her voice.

"I don't pretend to understand you."

Anable said softly, "No, don't, Geoffrey. Not about this, for I mean it. I'm happy right now, I . . ."

"Happy!" Geoffrey's voice rose threateningly. "Anable," he said, "I don't know what you're doing here anyway, I flew down tonight to . . ."

"Yes, why did you come down here, Geoffrey?"

Geoffrey's lips thinned angrily. "I think you're acting like a child. I think your actions are both crude and deplorable. When you change your mind, Anable . . ."

He snatched his hand away and left her standing in the center of the aisle. He did not look back; she could see him elbowing his way stubbornly through the crowds. She watched him as though she were in a trance, making no move to follow him. Her smile held a trace of irony. Of course I acted like a child, she thought. A lone unhappy tear slipped down her cheek; she might still run after Geoffrey, she could find a taxi and catch him at the airport, but she hesitated. In that moment of indecision she caught a glimpse of Jennie Margaret's head bobbing in the crowd below, straining to see her as she braved the flood of people very much like a salmon swimming upstream. Anable was curiously touched that she had been missed. Scrubbing her eyes with a handkerchief she waved at Jennie Margaret.

"I'm here," she shouted, and stepped cautiously down the bleacher steps.

But Jennie Margaret had stopped and was staring in fascination and surprise at a young man who was elbowing past her. Anable gave him a brief glance; he seemed a particularly unattractive young man but she did not wonder at Jennie Margaret's interest for his face was so bland and masklike that it resembled, oddly enough, an egg.

"What's the matter?" she asked Jennie Margaret.

"Why, I—I know that man," said Jennie Margaret,

frowning. "I've seen him somewhere but I can't remember when."

Anable said lightly, "It's a face not easily forgotten, if you ask me."

"But we've moved around so fast. Oh, Anable, I do know him. I have the feeling I've even talked to him. It's queer, not remembering."

Anable watched Jennie Margaret unconsciously rub her sleeve.

"Well, he's gone now. You're simply aging, Jennie Margaret. When you're as old as I am your memory will be worthless."

Jennie Margaret laughed. "I don't believe you. Why, Anable, where's Geoffrey?" She glanced around her, bewildered.

Anable was surprised at her own gentleness. "He was late for his plane, he had to run."

It satisfied Jennie Margaret. She placed her hand in Anable's and said confidingly, "I suppose he told you. I hope you're not angry, I do hope so, Anable. About the letter, I mean."

"About what letter?" Anable stopped and confronted Jennie Margaret. "What letter?" she asked sternly.

"Why, the letter I wrote to him, telling him where you were."

"I have not been my usually perceptive self," remarked Anable with grimness. "Jennie Margaret, let me remind you once again that all women are fools. Beware of it."

She no longer felt any inclination toward tears. If she

had wondered what enchanting whim had brought Geoffrey to her side Jennie Margaret's words settled it. Her letter, pale blue with kittens on it, had summoned him. It was quite probable that, like everyone else, Geoffrey believed Anable fully equipped to take care of herself.

"He could have at least worried," she brooded. "He could have fussed a bit. I might have been kidnapped, I might have been killed or—or—"

Jennie Margaret was staring at her in wonder. "Come along, Jen," she said aloud firmly, "it's our last night. It's party night. Tomorrow we begin our travels."

Something of Jennie Margaret's excitement crept into Anable so that her eyes were shining as they approached Harry Olsen's trailer. If her heart had been chipped, at least it was swiftly mended.

THEY arose early the next morning for there was much
to be done. Although nothing was said, a new spirit had
crept into the Caravan, a muted gaiety like the first
strains of an orchestra before a long-anticipated performance.

To Jeremy, awakening at dawn, it seemed irrelevant
that his circus work had ceased. He rolled over on his
side where, from the roof of the cabin he could just
glimpse the city below, gray and quiet, its street lamps
pale against the swimming light of dawn. The line of
mountains in the west was clear and fine, like a paper
cutout, with the great orange sun rising from below.

Jeremy yawned and wriggled his toes luxuriously.

Below him Jennie Margaret opened her eyes and sat up; she could feel the dawn, the taste and the smell of it, like a tangible thing. She leaned from the window, her face scrubbed and shining.

"Anable," she cried. "Wake up and feel it. We're leaving today!"

It was a holiday feeling, this new spirit, and one of security against the perils without, for there is insecurity in the making of new friends, but quietly, stealthily, Jeremy's last evening with Farnum and Zailey had made them old friends. It was this knowledge that caused them to smile warmly at one another over the breakfast table, and laugh at almost nothing.

The white quick-drying paint, recommended to them especially by the President of the Chamber of Commerce, had dried at noon. As Reuben pointed out, it gave them Class. The Caravan was now a creamy, lustrous white from stern to stern, punctuated crisply by red shutters and a toy flower box at each window; within a few hours she had become a prima donna of the road.

"I can't paint any of them fairies and guh-nomes you want," sighed the sign painter who had finished lettering *Candy Caravan, Inc.* on both doors. "But I know a fellow who can do it for you real cheap. Artist fellow."

"Hmm?" murmured Anable, frowning over a geranium she was planting in the window box. "Well, bring him around, will you? We plan to leave this afternoon." She removed her gloves and stepped back to study the Caravan with a professional eye. "Tell him we want something simple, neat but not gaudy. Just a border of elves at the base of the bus."

The sign painter sniffed disagreeably. "Some nice advertisements would catch the eye, lady." He was paid by the inch.

Anable gave him a frigid glance. "No," she said, "and I'd appreciate it if you'd hurry your artist friend over here."

As the painter ambled away, a truck drew up beside the Caravan and Jeremy leaped from its running board. "I got the refrigerator stalls, Anable. Reuben back yet with the ice cream?"

"Not yet, Mr. Peel. But the candy, chewing gum and cones are here."

Jennie Margaret wandered from the Caravan, sucking on a cherry lollipop. "Lunch is ready," she said. "Hello, Father."

"No time for lunch," shouted Jeremy. "Open up the rear doors and we'll get these installed. Is the dynamo here?"

"No," replied Anable.

"Yes," said Jennie Margaret. "It came while you were fetching the sign painter. It's all connected, he said to tell you."

With a screeching of brakes another truck halted beside the Caravan; it proved to be Reuben with the ice cream. "Hello," he called, "I'm back."

"Stars and garters!" cried Jeremy. "The ice cream already? Come, we must hurry!"

With a smile, Anable returned to her flowers and the

problem of coaxing a six-inch geranium stalk into four inches of soil. Presently a discreet cough reached her ears and she turned with a sigh, expecting, perhaps, the sign painter with whom she had waged battle.

But it was not the sign painter. It was, without a doubt, the artist whom he had recommended, or so Anable judged after a hasty glance at his clothing which was liberally daubed with the primary colors. He was a very tall, thin young man who carried himself with old-fashioned imperiousness. As their glances met the artist swept off his hat with a vast but wearied gallantry. It was a very dirty old hat.

"Jamie Falloden at your service," he announced.

"Anable Lea at *your* service," she said, and impulsively courtsied.

Mr. Falloden smiled gently.

"We wanted elves," Anable explained. "This is a Candy Caravan, as you can see. Isn't it a honey?"

Mr. Falloden's trained glance flicked over the bus and she could see that he approved.

"Can you manage the elves for us?"

"I'm sure that I can, Miss Lea." He placed his paint-box on the ground and extracted a pencil from his pocket. Then, without another word, he began scribbling illegible hieroglyphics at the base of the Caravan until Anable, wholly baffled, returned to her geraniums. They worked side by side until Anable, realizing that she was in the way, tiptoed discreetly back into the bus.

"The elves are being painted," she told Jennie Margaret with satisfaction. "Good job, too."

"Why didn't you tell me?" cried Jennie Margaret, and with great zest ran out to watch. "Hello," she said, and stopped. "Why, they're just darling!"

Mr. Falloden smiled gratefully. "You're very kind. But allow me to confide in you that I'm having a bit of trouble."

Jennie Margaret tore her gaze from the row of elves that had been blocked out roughly. "Trouble?" she repeated. "With them? But they look just like elves. All elves have turned up toes and pointed caps. And you've got them dancing nicely."

"But my elves have no faces," pointed out Mr. Falloden. "What sort of features would you suggest?"

"That's easy," laughed Jennie Margaret. "Big bright eyes, that's what they have; and funny little noses and thin mouths that smile."

Mr. Falloden was pleased. "That's exactly what I thought, but I'm glad you agree. Would you mind standing still for a few moments?"

"Me?"

"You," he assured her. "You will be my elf."

Jennie Margaret wriggled with excitement but she kept her face very still until Mr. Falloden, with great skill, had painted in Jennie Margaret's wide eyes and happy mouth.

"There!" he said. "Now I have a face for my elves."

"You mean all of them will look just like me?" She stood very close to Mr. Falloden and tried to look as professional as he as they glanced over the dancing parade.

"Some of them will have smaller eyes or longer noses,"

said Mr. Falloden, "but the look of mischief and the curve of the lips are exactly right. There will be a touch of you in them all."

Jennie Margaret's gaze flew to the long line of figures. "There are so many," she said anxiously.

He understood perfectly. Dipping his brush in yellow he drew in a small star beneath her picture. "There," he explained. "Now you will be able to find *your* elf."

"Oh," squealed Jennie Margaret, "I have a gold star just like Lucy." She enveloped Mr. Falloden in what was unquestionably a hug, and ran to tell Anable that she was a Caravan elf.

Jeremy, packing away the ice cream in the back of the Caravan, was suddenly startled at the sight of a strange head moving up and down outside of his window. Curious, he opened the double doors, arranged the steps and dismounted. He was further taken aback at the sight of the pixies parading over the Caravan, but even more so at Mr. Falloden with his eyes screwed together ominously, and a streak of crimson paint across his cheek. Jeremy stepped back and surveyed the decorations.

"Say, good job you're doing there," he cried, his eyes kindling with interest. "They look real lifelike!"

Mr. Falloden finished the left eye of his thirty-second elf and turned to observe his protagonist. "I'm happy you like it."

"I do, I do. You paint the letters, too?"

"No, I was brought in just for the elves. I'm an artist. I paint landscapes, figures, portraits."

"Is that so," commented Jeremy. "Well, now, that's very interesting, I've heard of people like you. Much money in painting?"

He thought a muscle tightened in the artist's jaw. "No," said Mr. Falloden. "Not for me, at any rate. If there were, I wouldn't be doing jobs like this."

Jeremy bridled. "Candy Caravan's going to make a lot of money," he said coldly. "We may even get to Florida in her, you know. Lots of money being spent down there."

Mr. Falloden gave Jeremy an indifferent glance and started his thirty-third elf.

"I don't like that painter fellow doing the elves," said Jeremy later, as they sat down to lunch. "He doesn't speak up, and when he does he hasn't a kind word to say. Don't care for people like that."

"Did you see the elves?" asked Jennie Margaret eagerly. "Did you notice how they resemble me?"

Jeremy was startled. "Why you?" he asked.

Anable explained. "She posed for them. You'll find a yellow star under the original."

"Well, I'll be interested in seeing that," said Jeremy. He frowned. "But later, when the painter chap's gone, if you don't mind. Like I said I didn't care for his attitude."

"He seemed exceptionally harmless," said Anable.

"Painters live romantic lives," Jennie Margaret announced, making hissing noises over her alphabet soup. "I've read lots about them. They live in places called garrets."

Reuben wrinkled his nose. "They're sissies."

At the sink, where she was tossing a salad, Anable said reproachfully, "I used to be an artist, and Mr. Peel, you're an artist, too, if of a different variety. You should be ashamed of yourself."

"I'm not," grumbled Jeremy.

"Were you really an artist?" asked Reuben. "I didn't know that, Anable."

She laughed. "It's a very misquoted word. Nowadays there are too many artists and not enough art."

Reuben glanced hopefully at the clock. "What time do we leave? Gosh, I wish you'd let me drive a little sometime. I could help both of you and get so experienced I could get a license."

"Don't be so piggish, Reuben," admonished Jennie Margaret. "Who would play dominoes or checkers with me if you drove?"

"Fight it out," smiled Anable, slipping off her apron. "I'm going out to pay Mr. Peel's mortal enemy."

"Give him a wooden nickel," chuckled Jeremy, pleased at his wit.

Jennie Margaret looked up sharply. "A wooden nickel?" she repeated. She slid off her chair and surreptitiously followed Anable outside. "Please don't, Anable," she whispered fiercely. "Father didn't know what he was saying. Really, the elf was wonderful. I think Mr. Falloden is super."

Anable squeezed her arm. "Don't worry," she said. "Mr. Falloden will receive every consideration, believe me, and no wooden nickels."

Anable found Mr. Falloden cleaning his brushes in turpentine. He seemed tired, but when he saw her he straightened and said quickly, "The elves won't dry for several hours. You'll have to be careful or they'll smudge."

Anable brushed this aside impatiently. "I brought you some cucumber sandwiches," she told him.

Mr. Falloden looked at Anable earnestly before he accepted the proffered sandwiches and devoured them. "I love them," he explained apologetically.

"You mean you haven't had your lunch," she corrected. "Tell me, Mr. Falloden, what do you do here in Pittsfield? Do you find, uh, good pickings here?"

"Well, not exactly. No, Miss Lea, in the summer I have a few students at a dollar an hour, and once in awhile someone asks me to do a portrait or desires a landscape as a Christmas present for an aunt. But—"

"Are you married?"

"No, I paint in bachelor splendor."

"Well, why in the world don't you go to New York?"

Mr. Falloden smiled shyly; his capable hands fluttered. "That is an honest question which I realize demands an honest answer, Miss Lea. You see, I am a failure. But I am also an artist, even though my foolish hands will not bring me success. As to why I do not go to New York, Miss Lea, a man who is a failure has the right to choose the place in which he can most happily fail. I do not like New York."

"A very honest answer," replied Anable. "What kind of work do you do?"

111

"I have a canvas with me in my paintbox. I worked on it early this morning. Would you care to see it?"

"I would," admitted Anable.

He brought it out carelessly, as if to disown it, yet at the same time his touch was tender. "It is 'Morning,'" he explained.

"It certainly is," breathed Anable.

Anable had moved in many an artistic circle but she had never seen anything like the canvas she held in her hands. It was the work of a man who had not ceased to think or feel but who had renounced all but a few influences and at last allowed nothing to pour from his brush but his own individuality. There was charm and strength in the painting, and a pattern that went deeper than decorativeness. It held a curiously haunting quality.

"Great guns," said Anable hotly, "I don't know why you're not famous. I think this stuff is unique."

She had the pleasure of seeing Mr. Falloden blush.

"Look here, Mr. Falloden," she said suddenly, placing her hands on her hips. "How would you like a trip south?"

"I beg your pardon?" and Mr. Falloden's blush deepened.

"It's this way," began Anable, unaware of his confusion. "There are four of us in the Caravan, and the rather surprising part of it is that until several weeks ago we had never before laid eyes upon one another, with the exception, of course, of Jennie Margaret and Mr. Peel. Jennie Margaret lived in an orphanage, and

Reuben worked in a garage, while I was out of a job."

"But now," went on Anable softly, "strange things are beginning to happen to us. You might almost say that each of us, in his own way, is becoming a potential success. Mr. Peel has become a clown again. Jennie Margaret has a father whom she adores, and Reuben is turning into a young man of confidence and consequence. Can you see what I mean?"

"And what has happened to you?" inquired Mr. Falloden with interest.

Anable laughed. "I am turning into a—a person," she said shyly. "Also a hostess, as you can see. Will you join us, Mr. Falloden?"

Mr. Falloden gazed at her deeply. "It is my turn to ask an honest question," he said. "Why should you ask me to join you?"

She smiled wistfully. "Because I believe you are unhappy; because I have itching fingers and cannot leave careers alone, which is why I am a press agent. And, why, because I like you."

"The last I appreciate the most," said Mr. Falloden gratefully.

"Then you'll come?" cried Anable.

Mr. Falloden smiled fully for the first time, and his smile was singularly sweet.

"If you will postpone your journey," he said, "until I may pack my suitcase and my paints."

WHEN Jennie Margaret heard that Mr. Falloden was to join them she said, "Oh, Anable, how *nice!*" But Jeremy gasped, "Stars and garters, why?"

Nor did his attitude toward the man mellow as they began their travels, for Jeremy refused to accept Mr. Falloden's arrival amongst them with equanimity. For him, the gaiety of their journey was gone.

His unexpected antagonism deepened into jealousy as he noticed how happily the others embraced and wel-

comed Mr. Falloden. Reuben, who had pronounced all
artists to be sissies, now held intricate conversations
with Mr. Falloden about baseball, sometimes continuing
the discussions far into the night, so that Jeremy was
forced to lie atop the Caravan and listen to their voices
across the roof. His own daughter treated the intruder
with affection and spent long hours explaining to him
her current problems. As for Anable, she had invited the
man.

So Jeremy sulked and brooded in a manner quite
strange to him; after all, he told himself, it was his Caravan and Mr. Falloden had no right to jeopardize his
position of masculine authority. Yet at the same time
there was shame in his heart that he acted in this fashion,
for he saw that had they met under different circumstances Jeremy would have liked Mr. Falloden and been
proud of his friendship. He especially approved the elf-
like drawing of Jennie Margaret which, although only a
hasty sketch, contained all the qualities that made Jennie Margaret so endearing to them all. Yet the crust of
shame and pride stiffened in Jeremy, and though he
knew that it troubled everyone, it was like a festering
splinter that he could neither draw out nor heal.

If there was disunity within the Caravan, the omnibus
itself carried them along more smoothly than ever before, its motor not at all temperamental and its products
a delight to every village. They drew close to New York
City with regret on Jeremy's part, for, being no longer
himself, he was tortured by all manner of forebodings.
He envisioned the Caravan smashed into a thousand

pieces by the wanton traffic of the great city or, worse yet, saw Anable snatched from them by the people she held spellbound in New York.

"We could go around the big town," he suggested hopefully one night, when they had drawn up on the parkway outside of Tuckahoe. He pointed with his finger at the map. "We could by-pass it altogether."

"Oh, Father," cried Jennie Margaret, "and miss New York? Why, I've never been there!"

"Of course you must see it," insisted Anable. She glanced objectively at Jennie Margaret and said, "She needs new clothes, Mr. Peel."

Jeremy looked with surprise at his daughter. He was quite accustomed to seeing her in the green uniform of the orphanage; now, examining her critically for the first time, he noticed that despite the brightly camouflaging touches that Anable had engineered, Jennie Margaret's frock remained, undeniably, a uniform. He was angry that he had not seen this for himself.

"Of course she must have new clothes," he replied. "But surely we can buy them anywhere."

"Why not compromise?" suggested Mr. Falloden firmly. "I understand Mr. Peel's concern thoroughly. It would be a pity to endanger the Caravan." But if he hoped for a rewarding glance from Jeremy he was disappointed, for Jeremy chose instead to regard the floor with such fervor as to startle them all.

Once again they pored over the little clothbound book into which Reuben was allowed to enter their day's earnings, and Anable to itemize them. They turned high the wick of the kerosene lamp and clustered around the bunk upon which Anable sat like a young priestess. When she had checked their wealth on paper she divided it into five equal parts and regarded it uneasily.

"I believe we eat too much," she said.

"Why, no," said Mr. Falloden, "the meagerness of the sum is due entirely to the fact that you have divided it by five."

"She can have my fifth," growled Jeremy, "it goes without saying. Every cent of it."

"Of course," smiled Mr. Falloden kindly, "but that is not the way to consider the problem. There are indeed four of you, and I do not count myself for I have newly joined your ranks, but can you possibly divide human beings by four? There is no method in the world by which this can be done properly. It is the four of you together who are making the Caravan a success. Why not leave the money alone? It is a fairly large sum when not divided, just as the four of you together are of much greater importance to the world than each of you individually."

It was a pity that he did not see Jeremy's admiring glance; at that moment Jeremy would have enjoyed shaking him stoutly by the hand.

"That's fine," said Anable slowly, "but if we spend it all tomorrow then we may need it suddenly the next day."

"Well," said Jeremy, "you must again find a way in which we can earn money." He grinned. "Surely *you* can find a way?"

117

Anable's laugh warmed them all. She put away the book and tousled Jennie Margaret's hair playfully. "We shall sleep on it," she decided.

But Jeremy did not sleep the whole night; he considered Mr. Falloden and the error of his ways. He longed to make amends yet at the same time he was shy of offering himself in vain.

"He's a good chap," he told himself, "with fine stuff in him. He says the words we all think but he arranges 'em in the right order. A bit stiff, a little too quiet but when he speaks, he's got something to say."

In the morning, after breakfast, Jeremy took Jennie Margaret and Reuben aside. "I've an idea," he explained. "We've no right to worry Anable by spending all our money in New York. Women are cautious, with a thought for tomorrow, and I confess I've leanings the same way."

"What do you plan?" asked Jennie Margaret excitedly. "Is it fun?"

He nodded solemnly, and from the trunk brought out his clown suits. "New Yorkers need more than a red and white caravan to make 'em want ice cream. I figgered maybe you and me and Reuben could dress up as clowns. Be a mite showier. Make us a little extra money. Think you could manage it?"

Jennie Margaret jumped up and down and pulled the clothes from Jeremy's hand. "They're lovely," she breathed. "Oh, Anable," she cried, "listen to Father's wonderful idea!"

They spent an hour over the wigs and makeup, laughing and shrieking and leering at one another. When they were dressed, Mr. Falloden coasted the omnibus into the very center of Tuckahoe, near the Town Hall, and then from the Caravan burst the three clowns. In their gaudy, comfortable clothes there was no necessity for caution, and what Jennie Margaret and Reuben lacked in skill they made up for in liveliness. Like three Pied Pipers they led the children and parents of Tuckahoe into the square, and as the high summer sun grew warmer the cash register rang all the more merrily.

"But why didn't we do this before?" cried Jennie Margaret, out of breath after turning four cartwheels in a row.

Anable smiled over her head at Jeremy. "It's just for special times, isn't it?" she said. Jeremy returned her smile and even included Mr. Falloden in its radius, but Reuben and Mr. Falloden had their backs turned as they busily scooped ice cream from the buckets and turned them into dripping pyramids.

"It's nice, being vagabonds," Anable added, with just a trace of wistfulness, for she would not have minded turning a few somersaults herself.

At noon Jennie Margaret and Reuben retreated to the cool sanctuary of the Caravan, not because their audience had diminished but rather because their energy was spent.

"Why don't we go to New York this afternoon?" asked Reuben, with an eye on the mound of silver they had earned. Jeremy also regarded it lovingly as though he had himself coined it. "You go along," he said generously,

"I'll tend the Caravan. We may as well make hay while the sun shines."

"You stay?" cried Jennie Margaret, shocked, "Oh, no, Father!"

Jeremy hesitated. He really preferred to remain, but at the same time he did not know how to insist upon it without hurting their feelings. New York appalled him with its subways that plunged pell-mell in a thousand directions. He had a weakness for quiet and order and it seemed to him that New York divested a man of both. "I really want to stay," he said, and hoped they would not feel obligated to persuade him. "I'll buy in more ice cream and have supper waiting when you come home."

They went, the four of them, leaving Jeremy behind.

They honestly intended to separate at Times Square, Mr. Falloden to visit the art galleries and Reuben to find his way by subway to the baseball park. But somehow, as they felt the pulse of the city squandering itself about them, it seemed exciting to be together, safe within their own circle of gaiety.

"I think I'll shop with you and Anable," said Reuben suddenly. "May I? Would it be all right?"

Mr. Falloden sighed in relief. "May I, too?" he asked, and they all laughed for no reason at all, so that passersby turned to stare at them curiously.

Arm in arm they marched away to the stores. It was Jennie Margaret's afternoon. When they had been shown to the proper department for young ladies' wear she was enraptured at the mannequins placed like giant paper dolls all over the floor.

"Oh," she cried, "did you ever see so many pretty clothes? I just wish Lucy could see them! But," she added soberly, "how expensive they all must be." She paused before an ugly calico dress, having succeeded in reading the price tag by peering at it upside down. She admired it with elaborate politeness.

"No," said Mr. Falloden resolutely, "that absolutely won't do."

"Absolutely," said Reuben, elevated by Mr. Falloden's presence in this bewilderingly feminine world.

"It must be attacked like a painting," stated Mr. Falloden with decision, "for our Jennie Margaret is certainly as attractive and colorful as any to be seen." Clasping Jennie Margaret's hand in his, he led her away from Anable and toward a rack of soft, vivid cotton frocks. "Here," he said, selecting one. "As crisp as a peppermint stick. Just the thing."

They were startled when Jennie Margaret appeared in it, and so inspired by the change in her appearance that even Reuben entered with zest into the venture. When the afternoon had grown long and they left the store to sip lemonades in a drugstore, each of them had selected at least one article for Jennie Margaret's new wardrobe. Now she could boast a striped afternoon frock, a Sunday dress the color of ripe mangoes, a plaid sun suit, a navy blue cape, and a pair of sturdy dungarees for play. They returned to the Caravan exhausted but filled with stories of Mr. Falloden's prowess in shopping, his views on color and size, and his bewitching air with shopgirls.

121

Jeremy, who had helped them earn the money in the only manner in which he knew, who had missed them painfully all afternoon and been prepared to include even Mr. Falloden in his warm welcome, felt bitterly neglected. He had not shared an adventure that would linger long as a memory. He went to bed feeling very cross and did not fall asleep until he had reassured himself that although his Caravan lay in strange hands it belonged legally to him.

The rift between the two men had deepened. It took, in fact, the President of the United States to bring them together.

They found Washington slumbering heavily in a quiet dawn, exhausted from lobbyists, strikes and foreign incidents. Its streets gave off a cloud of steam under the hoses of the invading utility workers whose blatant voices were for a few hours the only speech to be heard in a city of words.

The Caravan came from the north, fresh from a night spent beside the Potomac. The morning differed from no other except that Reuben was driving, which made it an exceedingly adventuresome day for him. Anable sat beside him in her new role of assistant, while Jennie Margaret hovered between them, not quite trusting the Caravan to either and yet silently worshiping them both.

To Jeremy had fallen the job of refilling the empty racks of candy and chewing gum, and it became apparent almost from the moment they entered Washington that his companion would be Mr. Falloden. They worked together without a word, but Mr. Falloden allowed himself the luxury of whistling softly. He whistled *Danny Boy*, which he knew to be a great favorite of Jeremy's. At the end of the song he managed a fine trill but when no comment was forthcoming he subsided, despite the fact that he would have liked to go on to *Annie Laurie.*

"Lovely buildings, eh?" he hazarded, staring out of the window.

"Oh, yes," Jeremy replied coolly, but he surreptitiously glanced over Mr. Falloden's shoulder. He would have loved to confide his many thoughts on the wonder of passing through his nation's capital, but pride pressed him into silence.

From the front of the bus came a joyous cry from Jennie Margaret. "The White House, Father. See the White House!"

Jeremy could no longer conceal his excitement. He sprang to the window and thrust out his head.

"Stars and garters!" he exclaimed. "It's the White House! Just like the pictures!"

"Exactly like," murmured Mr. Falloden.

The Caravan came to a halt, and it was then that Jeremy saw the President.

The President of the United States stood beside the gate of the White House, very straight and trim in his double-breasted suit. There were Secret Service men on either side of him, but the President was paying them no attention. He was staring straight at the provocative vision of Candy Caravan, Inc. loitering beside the curb.

"Mr. Falloden," whispered Jeremy. "It's the President!"

Just then the President saw Jeremy and smiled. "Do you have any vanilla ice cream?" he called.

Jeremy nodded.

The President took a dime from his pocket. "I'd like a vanilla cone," he said, grinning.

"A vanilla cone," cried Jeremy. "Oh, yes, Mr. President!"

With shaking hands he accepted the cone that Mr. Falloden thrust at him, and made the President of the United States an enormous vanilla ice-cream cone.

"You have a remarkable bus here," said the President, watching him through the window.

"We're going south in it," said Jeremy breathlessly. "We may even get to Florida."

"Will you now," said the President. "Well," he went on with a twinkle, "if you decide to go to Missouri instead, tell them I'll be down for some fried chicken just as soon as the Republicans will let me."

Jeremy handed him the cone; at the same moment a surprising idea occurred to him. He remembered Herb Bowler, how learned and wise he had seemed, yet how troubled, and Jeremy thought the President might feel the same way. "Just a minute, Mr. President," he whispered excitedly and reached deep into a nearby drawer. "I'd like to give this to you, sir."

And Jeremy stared long and earnestly at the President, hoping that he would understand the gift of the book entitled *How To Get Along With The Russians.*

The President glanced at the book and smiled. "Why, thank you, my friend." Thrusting his arm through the window he shook Jeremy's hand warmly.

"We're with you," cried Jeremy. "Don't you forget it, sir."

As the President walked through the gates of the White House Jeremy wiped his forehead.

"Stars and garters," he groaned. "I'll bet that was a stupid thing—the stupidest thing ever—to give the President of the United States. I guess I'm the biggest fool in this country."

He looked in agony into the face of his sworn enemy, Mr. Falloden. He could have withstood scorn or contempt, he even anticipated it, but at Mr. Falloden's words his resistance crumbled.

"I think it was a fine thing to do," said Mr. Falloden gently. "A very heart-warming gesture for a President of the United States."

He and Jeremy smiled at each other. They were friends at last.

THE Caravan cruised into Virginia, its five occupants in a mellowed, beneficent mood. Their ledger book showed a pretty array of figures which, if not startling, was soothing to their sense of security and allowed them to purchase a tarpaulin for the roof dwellers, a new tire for the Caravan, and a pair of shoes for Mr. Falloden. This last was suggested by Jeremy almost immediately following their stop in Washington, and by this move everyone realized that the proverbial hole in their dike had been mended. Mr. Falloden was very pleased to toss aside his ragged sneakers.

The late June sun was hot and though this evil was, of necessity, a boon to business, the Caravan slackened its pace accordingly and their life became increasingly gypsylike.

"It's this way," expounded Anable pleasantly, her thoughts of commerce tentatively diminished as she sunbathed on the roof of the Caravan. "One can spend a lifetime making money, but so what? There is no time in which to spend the money. It is a vicious circle, isn't it? What we must discover is *how to work and spend in moderation.* It is, obviously, the only solution."

"That sounds most attractive," said Mr. Falloden lazily, "but I have worked hard all my life and at the same time had no money to spend. How can you reconcile that? Everything," he concluded, with a wink at Jeremy, "seems to be relative."

He and Jeremy beamed at one another with complete understanding. There was not a moment of the day when they did not understand each other now, and prove it by a wink, a glance, a slight tipping of the head. They were almost disgustingly chummy, thought Anable.

"Relative or not," she said, rolling over on her stomach, "the fact remains you didn't have me around then. I can do anything."

"Can you really, Anable?" asked Mr. Falloden.

Anable laughed. "Of course," she said. "It's my byline, my motto. Jennie Margaret, what are you up to now?"

A smaller edition of Anable had moved into the fields before their eyes. It was Jennie Margaret, wearing a sun suit that exactly matched the one Anable wore.

"Just playing catch with Reuben," she called back. "It's all he wants to do, Anable."

Her underlip was quivering, but Anable and Jeremy were too far away to see this. Jennie Margaret did not like to play catch with Reuben; the hard ball stung her fingers when she caught it, and her shoulder ached from returning it. But she worshiped Reuben, as she worshiped all of them, and deep within her she yearned to be as important to them as they were to her.

"Where do you want me today?" she called. "Where, Reuben?"

"Right there," Reuben shouted from a distance. His arm extended sharply, casting a grotesque shadow across the ground, and a neatly curved ball shot toward her, hard and straight as a pebble. Flinching, Jennie Margaret caught it.

"It's no hot potato," shouted Reuben irritably. "Toss it back. Give it a good heave."

Jennie Margaret gritted her teeth and returned it to him clumsily.

"Oh, for Heaven's sake," exhorted Reuben. "Don't they ever teach girls how to throw?"

"N-no," whimpered Jennie Margaret, nobly blinking away her tears. She watched as Reuben went through a series of exaggerated movements that he called a wind-up. The ball whistled as it cut the air near Jennie Margaret and she let it fly past her, running quickly to pluck it from the grass before Reuben noticed her inadequacy.

She heard his voice rather than his words; he sounded very angry. She turned and cried out, "Reuben, please . . ." but he was running away from her with long strides, heading for the woods at the edge of the field. She did not know what to do; she had made a mistake that displeased him and now there was nothing to do but follow. With a sigh she started after him.

Reuben was not angry with her. To her great surprise she found that he was sobbing. As she walked up to him he tried desperately to hide his tears, cradling his face in the sanctuary of his arms. "Go away, Jennie Margaret," he cried, "go away, I tell you."

She stood before him, perplexed. It was frightening and she wanted to leave but her feet would not carry her away. "Please, Reuben, please don't cry," she whispered, and saw that she had said exactly the wrong words.

Reuben lifted his wet face angrily. "Will you get out of here?" he said threateningly.

"No," shouted Jennie Margaret with an anger that matched his own. "No, I won't. I won't. I won't, and you have no right to talk to me like this. What makes you this way?"

"You wouldn't understand," Reuben said. "You're only thirteen years old."

"I know a great deal," Jennie Margaret told him tartly, "and I'm going to be fourteen in only a few months. I don't know why you have to be high-horsey, Mr. Malone. You grew up at the same place that I did."

"But you have a father," Reuben pointed out bitterly. "You have a father and a Caravan, and people to take care of you. I haven't anything, not even a pitching arm."

"A pitching arm! But what . . . ?" Jennie Margaret bit her lip; it occurred to her that this might be important to Reuben. "Is that what you want, Reuben? Is that why you're crying?"

"Maybe," he said. "Maybe that and other things."

"Well, that's nothing," she said confidently. "That's something that only takes practice. Why," she went on excitedly, trying to remember all that Anable said in cases like this, "why, you're just made to be a pitcher." She ran her eyes over him covertly. "Pitchers are—well, they're just your height, and they weigh exactly what you do, and all pitchers have blue eyes and sandy hair, honest they do. And . . ."

Reuben's lips curved into a smile. "Oh, Jen," he sighed, "you're good, like your father. How I wish I could always stay with you."

"Well, why not?" gasped Jennie Margaret. "We're all going to be together just always."

His fingers dug into the grass fiercely. "No, we won't. Life doesn't happen that way. Your father's been swell, but he won't want me around forever. This is—well, it's just a vacation."

"You mean we won't always belong together and be a family?" Jennie Margaret's gaze was wide and incredulous.

"It's because you're thirteen," said Reuben with authority. "Although almost fourteen," he amended, seeing her face fall. "I'm seventeen, I know grownups through and through. We're only a novelty to Anable, she'll forget about us soon; the trip is a vacation for Falloden, but he's got a philosophy, he'll be at home anywhere. Your father—well, this is his Caravan and he'll always have it, and you're a real daughter to him now, Jennie Margaret, I can see it when he looks at you. I'm just a runaway."

"From Gallup Corners?"

"Yes." His gaze was far away, as it was many evenings when he was tired or thinking hard. Jennie Margaret leaned over and patted his hand.

"Reuben," she said simply, "please be happy. Please like me, for I like you tremendous. And we *will* be together. Reuben, we *will*."

He smiled and squeezed her hand. "That's a pact, Jennie Margaret. Will you remember it no matter what happens?"

Jennie Margaret had no idea what he meant, but from the depths of her heart she responded to the loneliness in his voice. "And can we need each other a little?" she asked gravely. "Like a brother and sister?"

"A great deal," he told her solemnly, and they shook hands.

"I'm glad," Jennie Margaret cried. "Isn't this nice? And I'll be your catcher any day," she told him eagerly. "I'll be your catcher anytime at all, Reuben; honest I will."

"I think it must hurt your hand," Reuben said in perfect understanding. "Your hands are pretty small, Jennie Margaret."

She held one out to him and he swung himself to his

feet. "I don't look as though I'd been crying?" he asked her, worried.

"Not at all!"

As they walked back to the Caravan Jennie Margaret unconsciously squared her shoulders. She had been recognized; she was at last important in someone else's eyes beside her own. It was a rapturous feeling. She could hardly wait to grow up.

So their June days were spent, lazily, with a good humor to which Jeremy contributed wisdom, Anable confidence, Mr. Falloden gentleness, and Jennie Margaret and Reuben a secret understanding compiled of good will and youth. Their first six weeks of Caravan life drew to a close.

ANABLE was restless.

There was always a moment in the various lives which Anable led when she yearned to discover what lay around the next corner. It was a feeling which in Anable amounted almost to a physical illness, so that when it attacked her she would rout it with characteristic zest by throwing her belongings into a suitcase, shutting the door behind her and entering into a new existence.

Under the present circumstances this was impossible and, lying prone on the bunk, Anable graciously admitted it. Although there was no reason why she could not walk to the cash register only a few feet away from her and extract from it the train fare to New York, she realized at the same time that she had allowed herself to become entangled, seriously so. What particularly

133

irked Anable was that she was not even entangled by A Man, but rather by two gentlemen of varying ages, a young boy and an even younger girl. For the first time in her life Anable was needed, was a fragment of a pattern that without her would tear and become many single threads. And she was rebellious.

Restlessly she stared from the window, snatching at ideas that occurred to her, sorting and pigeon-holing them. But she could not leave Jeremy, whom she loved for many reasons, nor Jennie Margaret to whom she was a princess, nor Reuben who accepted and admired her; not even Mr. Falloden whom she had herself invited. She was neatly, irrevocably trapped in a cage without bars. She sought now for a word with which she might amply express herself; there were none of her own but a familiar term sprang to her lips and she uttered it forcibly. "Nuts," she said simply, and relaxed.

"Why, Anable!" Jennie Margaret sat up straight in the rocking chair and laid aside her book. "Are you sick? Don't you feel well?"

Anable frowned. "Must I be sick? I'm merely tired."

Jennie Margaret turned pale. "Oh, Anable, of us? Of the Caravan?"

"You know better than that, Jen," said Anable with spirit. "On the contrary, I'm tired of myself."

Jennie Margaret was visibly relieved. "I don't understand," she said, "but it's all right. I was afraid . . ."

"You mustn't be." Anable sat up, slim and tousled, but curiously preoccupied so that Jennie Margaret felt shut out. She gave Jennie Margaret an absent glance. "It's quite possibly growing pains."

"Growing pains?" laughed Jennie Margaret. "But you're all grown up!"

Anable sighed. "No, I'm not. Everyone grows up crooked in some way or another."

"But how are you crooked, Anable? Please tell me."

She spread out her hands blindly. "I'm just learning about it. For one thing, I—I shirk responsibility."

"You?" cried Jennie Margaret. "But you've been managing all of us. You're a press agent."

Anable thought about this for a moment. "No, you're wrong, Jen," she decided. "You see, I never send down any roots, and that is a very important part of knowing both oneself and other people. It's like going to a cake sale and flitting from cake to cake tasting a few crumbs of each. I have bad habits, Jennie Margaret; I sample people just like cake. Then I move on. It means that I am never bored, but I am also crooked. Do you see what I mean?"

"Yes. But you've stayed with us, Anable."

She smiled. "For the first time in my life I'm breaking a bad habit. It's good for me, if a little distressing."

Jennie Margaret thought she understood. In the spring when all the girls at the orphanage were given caps and aprons she had yearned to be free as the wind to escape Miss Arbuckle's terrifying talks on responsibility. Perhaps Anable felt like that; her third finger had a blister from the stove and they all told her their troubles, whereas once she had known no one's troubles but her own.

"Oh, dear," thought Jennie Margaret, "if only Geoffrey were here." She stared anxiously out of the window and then all of a sudden she brightened. A little smile trembled at the corners of her mouth. From the sandy vistas of the road, which had hitherto yielded only Burma-Shave signs, there loomed a large banner which in bold red and blue letters announced to all the world that Wisteria City, Virginia, was celebrating the Fourth of July in the only fashion that it should be celebrated.

"Of course!" she decided. Anable must have a taste of bright lights, noise and diversion; it was exactly what was needed to cheer her up.

"See the signs?" she cried aloud. "Please let's stop. We'll celebrate the Fourth of July!"

She ran to Jeremy to tell him.

Wisteria City had no wisteria nor was it a city. It was a sprawling, dusty town with a few cottonwoods which the First Baptist Conservation of Trees Society had succeeded in preserving; a stately row of dying elms which the Civic Club had planted as a memorial to their first president; and a shabby regional high school. There were sections of it that suggested the town dated back to the War Between the States, tall-storied houses with graceful fan lights and no plumbing; but for the most part Wisteria City was comprised of raw new bungalows, without shade or grass or human dignity, and none of them older than the WPA.

Into this rolled Candy Caravan, Inc.

"I don't think much of this place," grumbled Jeremy. "If there's a Fourth of July celebration here it's because the town's just waked up. Like Rip Van Winkle."

But they followed the scarlet arrow to the fairgrounds and when they arrived there Jeremy could understand the emptiness of Wisteria City; the entire district had swarmed to the holiday festival; their cars were parked three deep around the entrance. Jeremy edged the Caravan into a slice of space beside the Arcade, and almost before he had locked the ignition they were surrounded by a horde of interested spectators.

"But we came to have fun," protested Jennie Margaret. "Oh, Father, do we have to sell ice cream?"

Jeremy smiled at Mr. Falloden and Mr. Falloden nodded. "I'll stay," he offered gallantly. "You go and watch the celebration."

Anable examined the crowd and sighed. "I'll help," she said. "You can't handle this crowd alone. I'd rather go tonight and see the fireworks, anyway."

Jennie Margaret hastened into the cabin to change into her best dress and hair ribbon, while Jeremy removed nickels and dimes from the cash register and placed them in his pocket. Presently he and Jennie Margaret and Reuben disappeared arm in arm, their eyes bright with anticipation.

Anable and Mr. Falloden worked tirelessly until the sun sank behind the shortest, stubbiest tree in Virginia. They passed out dripping cones until there was no longer any ice cream to be sold.

"Fifty-one dollars," said Anable, grimly counting the pennies and dimes. She pushed back her hair and tenderly removed her shoes. "Fifty-one dollars helps my aching feet, but not much."

"It's extraordinary that people buy so much ice cream," observed Mr. Falloden. "It seems a commodity that few people can live without, yet for years I never considered it among the scheme of things."

"I don't believe you considered food among your scheme of things, either," commented Anable. "You're beginning to look like a man who climbs into a suit instead of hanging it on."

Mr. Falloden laughed. "How right you are." He studied himself gravely. "In a few months I shall be as plump as any of my envied patrons. What surprises life has in store for us!"

"I'd like a few of the surprises for myself, if you don't mind," retorted Anable with a trace of bitterness.

"Ah, my dear Anable, I suspected as much. You're growing restless, aren't you?"

"Yes, I am," sighed Anable. "Is it that I'm getting old, Falloden? I think I begin to want security. I've spent years running away from it and now it's suddenly what my heart cries out for—a place in life, a bit of dignity, a few people I know well, a few that I love. Oh, but it sounds so depressing."

"On the contrary," said Mr. Falloden politely, "it is what each new generation has eventually discovered, my dear; and if it is why we older folks seem depressing to you, it is also why there *are* succeeding generations."

"Falloden, you sound very old," observed Anable.

Mr. Falloden smiled. "At times I feel very old."

"Then do I seem frightfully callow to you, Falloden?"

He made a gesture of impatience. "I envy your incredible interest in what lies around the next corner. It's fine and good to keep searching, my dear, because when you find what lies next to your heart it is permanent."

"I disagree with you," she replied bitterly. "If you search too long, nothing becomes permanent; it's just a habit. You're the lucky one, Falloden; you've found exactly what you want to do in life and you're happy." She sighed. "It must be so peaceful."

"Itching fingers?" he said gently. "You described yourself to me in that manner once."

"Yes. Weary, itching fingers, darn it." She tossed her shoes into the Caravan and stretched out her legs. "I don't think I'll go to the fireworks, after all; I'm sure I can see them from here. Did you plan to go?" she asked politely.

Mr. Falloden shook his head. "I shall sit and sketch," he decided.

"Excuse me," said a voice from the rear of the bus, "but do you have any ice cream for a hot, tired traveler?"

Anable whirled; leaning from a long, sleek, cream-colored convertible was a young man of equal sleekness, not at all hot or tired but obviously a traveler, as the bulging back seat of his car proclaimed. Under the stranger's prolonged glance Anable stiffened instinctively; she was not unfamiliar with his type, there was one in front of every cigar store on a Saturday night, but she had never before encountered one of the species face to face. She felt Falloden's presence beside her as a bulwark.

"I'm afraid we have not even a scraping left," said Mr. Falloden mildly. But the young man, having seen Anable, was not so easily discouraged. Slamming the door of his car he sauntered casually toward them, his smile solely for Anable, his eyes speculative. "Never thought I'd find a classy doll like you in this hole," he said, rudely ignoring Falloden. "Mind if I have a seat?" He spread a sheet of newspaper and sat down with a nod for the Caravan. "Saw your Pennsylvania license plate. I'm from New York and sure glad to meet some people without hayseed in their hair." The strange young man shot a look of contempt at Mr. Falloden. He was not as sure of himself as a moment ago but he was determined to elbow his way in nevertheless.

He was an excessively immaculate young man; none of Anable's friends had ever achieved such a crease in their trousers; no laundry of her acquaintance expelled such gleaming collars. But his face was incongruous— its flesh was stretched tightly as though it were pinned back behind his ears, and a strange half-smile twisted his mouth, never allowing it to relax. His nose, broken in several places, held Anable's attention until she realized that she was staring.

"As Mr. Falloden said," Anable remarked, "we're

completely out of ice cream." She smiled faintly not wishing to seem lacking in manners, but she could not keep her gaze from his smooth face, his startling pin-stripe suit or the luggage that lay in the back seat of his striking automobile. *I never forget a face,* she thought, *and I've glimpsed this man before.* He resembled a gangster or perhaps, life being what it is, only a poet with an inherited income.

With her words their new visitor gained confidence. "You got a quaint bus here," he said condescendingly. "Not bad at all. Me, I don't go for quaint things but they bring in dough. Not big dough, but enough. You been to the Fair yet?"

"No," said Mr. Falloden calmly.

"Police raided it yet?" He watched Anable closely and when she shrugged he brightened visibly. "Swell," he said, "guess I'll stick around." He adjusted the brim of his hat to a jauntier angle, stood up, and swaggered back to his car. But with one foot on the running board he paused and gave the Caravan a long stare.

"I've seen this buggy somewhere," he said. "Never forget a car, not me. Didn't look like this when I saw it, though—it's been spruced up."

"That's true," Anable agreed amiably. "Where did you see it before?"

The young man shrugged, gave Anable a smile, and climbed into his automobile.

"Well!" said Anable when he had driven away. "What do you think of him!"

"I," said Mr. Falloden, "found him quaint." They both

laughed and Anable looked over his shoulder into his sketchbook. "Why," she gasped, "you made a drawing of him. It's absolutely perfect," she cried.

But Falloden modestly closed his sketchbook. "We'll watch the fireworks now," he said, and sat back expectantly.

AT the far end of the midway three of the Caravanners stepped from the roller coaster feeling sadly subdued.

"My tummy hurts," confided Jennie Margaret.

Jeremy nodded. "You always eat too much, Jennie Margaret. Now you've made me eat too much. All that cotton candy, my, my."

"Well, but I've always wanted to go on a roller coaster, Father. I don't mean I'm sorry, I just mean I'm sick."

"Why don't we all sit down?" suggested Reuben.

They lowered themselves to the grass and hugged

their stomachs until the earth ceased its relentless spinning. Around them surged the crowds of men, women, and children, their faces pale under the arc lights and grimly intent upon extracting from the Fair its last measure of thrills.

"Could I try the shooting galleries now?" asked Reuben. "I could win something, maybe. I'd like to try."

"Here's some money," Jeremy said. "If you don't mind, I'm going to stay here. Sitting down is the best fun I've had at this Fair yet. How about you, Jennie Margaret?"

Jennie Margaret nodded. "I'll stay with you, Father."

They watched Reuben thread his way through the crowd. "He's a nice boy," Jeremy observed. "I'm growing real fond of him. He was old for his years at first, but the Caravan's giving him the fun he missed."

"I think he's wonderful, Father."

Suddenly Jeremy chuckled. "See that man over there, Jennie Margaret, right about where Reuben disappeared?"

"There's a lot of men over there, Father."

"I mean the one with the briefcase and the speckled bow tie."

"Oh, yes," replied Jennie Margaret. "Doesn't he look nice?"

"Well," said Jeremy, "I know him. Herb!" he shouted. "Mr. Bowler!"

Mr. Bowler stopped and turned around, his face puzzled. When he saw Jeremy he beamed. "Why, Mr. Peel!" he cried, and hastened over to them, his heels kicking up little clouds of sawdust behind him. "What a coincidence to meet again! Mr. Peel, I'm glad to see you."

"Meet my daughter, Jennie Margaret," said Jeremy with pride. "We've just been on the roller coaster."

"You've been on the roller coaster, have you? Well, well!"

"It was fun, the roller coaster," confided Jennie Margaret. "I'm going to be a trapeze artist when I grow up, you know."

Mr. Bowler sat down between them and stretched his legs. "She's a nice daughter," he said shyly. "You've stopped being a clown, Mr. Peel?"

Jeremy beamed. "Retired, Herb. Me and the Caravan and several friends of mine are going south. You look pretty good, Herb. You look like the books are selling real well."

Mr. Bowler's Adam's apple moved convulsively. "Well," he said, "Well, yes, I'm doing better." Then in a still, small voice, without looking at Jeremy he said, "I'm selling comic books, Mr. Peel."

Jennie Margaret cried, "Comic books? Oh, I love comic books!"

Both Jeremy and Herb surveyed her sadly. Jeremy shook his head. "That's too bad, Herb. You had to give it up?"

"I got money now, Mr. Peel," said Herb. "I've even got a little secondhand car and I don't have to hitch-hike any more. I got a new suit of clothes, too; green herringbone tweed, it is. I've got all a man could ask for, but the heart's gone out of me, Mr. Peel. I look at the way the

145

world's going and then I think of the American Public." Herb tightened his lips into a fretful line. "I just don't know."

They sat quietly on the grass, the radiant world of the carnival streaming about them, and they found nothing to say to each other. Then Jeremy brightened.

"That book you gave me," he said. "That book about the Russians you gave me."

Mr. Bowler glanced up.

"I gave it to the President," said Jeremy. "I thought you might like to know."

"The President?" repeated Mr. Bowler.

"Yes, sir; of the United States."

"The *President of the United States?*" Mr. Bowler's eyes widened in unconcealed awe. "You gave that book to the *President?*"

"Gave it to him with these two hands, and he said 'Thank you, my friend!' He's real pleasant, Herb; likes vanilla ice cream."

"Well, well," gasped Herb and stood up, a curious light dawning in his eyes. "Well, well, *well.*"

He stood very humbly before them, his hands open with the palms heavenward, as though he were absorbing a God-sent message that only he could interpret. Then, without saying another word, like a man in a blind trance, he moved slowly away from them and down the road.

"Is he all right?" whispered Jennie Margaret. "Where is he going? Why didn't he stay?"

As Mr. Bowler became swallowed up in the milling

crowd Jeremy smiled, for it seemed to him that Herb had again walked as though to the beat of celestial drums. "I think it's time to go home," Jeremy said quietly. "I think only Mr. Bowler knows where he's going."

About midnight a gentle rain began falling; regretfully the throngs began to disperse, veering toward their dusty cars or standing apathetically under huge, dripping umbrellas that blossomed magically like swollen flowers with drooping, human stems. The rain dampened Jennie Margaret and Jeremy miserably before they reached the Caravan, and further bedraggled Jeremy's Continental bow tie which he wore now for its sentimental associations.

Mr. Falloden and Anable had cocoa and crackers waiting for them; they had labored faithfully over the stove to surprise them.

It was Reuben who returned first, with a kewpie doll from whose face the paint had begun to run; then suddenly they were all in the Caravan, dwarfing the furniture and stumbling over one another like giants in a doll's house. They sat at the table glowing from their festivities, their faces shining and still damp. Outside, the rain pelted the windows urgently and there was a faint sound of thunder from a distance—the Caravanners rubbed their hands together and agreed that it was good to be home.

"Pull the curtains," advised Jeremy. "We've had enough of the carnival and this rain."

"It's pouring," said Anable, drawing together the crimson curtains.

"You can have the kewpie doll," Reuben told Jennie Margaret, suddenly aware that it was a doll and no longer a trophy to be carried conspicuously. "You can have it as a present."

"Well, thank you very much. But its face looks kind of funny, Reuben, and I'm getting a little old for dolls."

"I'll touch it up for you first thing in the morning," promised Mr. Falloden.

"We can sew a long skirt for it," suggested Anable, "and it will cover your bed during the day."

"Well, now," observed Jeremy, slouching deep into his chair and reaching with one arm for his steaming mug of cocoa. "This is the life, I say. Falloden, your cocoa is splendid; you're no mean cook."

"I followed directions to the word," replied Mr. Falloden drily. "They print them in large letters on the box; very thoughtful of them."

"What did you do tonight?" inquired Jennie Margaret of Mr. Falloden.

"Sketched." And Mr. Falloden told them of the young man who had stopped to talk to them.

"His face looked just like a painted eggshell," broke in Anable. "I'm quite sure he was a professional gambler."

"Does that please you?" asked Jennie Margaret in surprise.

Jeremy was shocked at her smile. "Anable, you don't enjoy criminals?"

Her smile became a laugh. "I enjoy everyone," she said. "Girls have to or they never discover anything about life. How else can you learn except through people themselves?"

"I don't believe Geoffrey would like to hear you talk that way," said Jennie Margaret, for whom there were no intermediate shades of gray in the scale of human behavior. "People are either good or bad. I don't pay any attention to the bad ones."

Possibly Anable might have answered Jennie Margaret, but there came at that moment a knock upon their door. It was an ordinary knock; there was nothing sinister or frightening about it to warn them, just a quiet rat-a-tat-tat to be heard above the storm outside. Jeremy laid down his cup of chocolate, gave a wry glance at his stockinged feet and said, "I'll go." He was, after all, nearest the door.

Someone, it was perhaps Falloden, remarked that it was a late hour for callers and Anable said yes, wasn't it, and they smiled and all of them drank up the last dregs of their cocoa.

"I'm sleepy," said Jennie Margaret, and her yawn made a tiny whine.

They heard Jeremy's startled grunt. Then a low murmur of voices rose from the doorway, as though in argument, and suddenly the curtains parted and they had a full view of their late guests.

They were two policemen.

Their raincoats glistened from the rain and their eyes were narrowed against the bright light, so that they seemed unusually menacing. Jeremy looked very small beside the bulk of them.

"Hello," Anable said gaily.

One of the policemen crossed to the table at which they sat and placed his hand on Reuben's shoulder. "You Reuben Malone?" he asked.

Reuben turned white. Anable said brightly, "What's the matter?" and then closed her mouth angrily, for no one paid her the slightest attention. Slowly, gradually, they all felt the first ominous chill of fear tightening the atmosphere, sucking at their breath like a great vacuum, draining from each corner the old echoes of their laughter. No one could speak; the clock ticked cheerfully on the shelf above the sink and the rain danced against the windows, but no one could say a word. They simply stared, all of them, at Reuben's terrified face.

"What do you want with him?" asked Anable at last in a small voice.

The policeman released Reuben's shoulder. "He's wanted in Vermont, ma'am. He's wanted for robbery."

The word had a bizarre ring to it as it burst upon the cozy, makeshift cabin of the Caravan. Jeremy said hoarsely, "That's not true! He's a good boy. Who could he have robbed, a young boy like him?"

"He's old enough to steal five thousand dollars," said the policeman grimly. "He slugged the guy he worked for up in Gallup Corners, Vermont, and disappeared the same day. A gas station man by the name of Harry Petrie."

"Gallup Corners?" repeated Anable.

"Petrie!" cried Jeremy. "Why, I know the man! But

Reuben couldn't have done a thing like that—it's the most ridiculous charge I've ever heard."

The policeman shrugged. "That's none of our business. We've been looking for him. Now we've found him. You ready, Malone?"

"I'll go," said Reuben, "it's all right, Mr. Peel. I'll go." His lips had begun to quiver; he crammed a fist against his mouth to steady them. He felt their probing glances, even their terror for him, but it seemed to Reuben that only Jennie Margaret's gaze withheld questions.

Jeremy was startled, as though aware of his own perfidy. Here they sat, staring curiously at Reuben, willing him to deny the charges with not a word of reassurance for him.

"He didn't do it, you know. He didn't do it," Jeremy announced flatly.

The two policemen crossed to Reuben and snapped handcuffs over his trembling wrists; he was a dangerous man now, and they were taking no chances. When Jennie Margaret saw them do this she screamed.

"Don't, Jennie Margaret," Reuben begged. "Please don't. I'll be back, honest."

"No, you won't!" cried Jennie Margaret. "You won't! Let him go, let him go, how dare you hurt him!"

"Now, now, Jennie Margaret," admonished Mr. Falloden, stroking her hair. "They won't hurt him."

"We'll go now," said the policeman. "He's got a long trip ahead of him."

But Jeremy resolutely gathered up his shoes and his raincoat. "I'm going, too," he declared angrily. "I'm not going to leave you, Reuben. We'll do something about this, boy—we'll fight them. I'm tired to death of just taking and taking; we'll fight hard. Mr. Falloden, take care of things, will you? I'm going to Gallup Corners."

"Yes, of course you're going," said Mr. Falloden serenely. "Good-bye for awhile, Reuben."

Reuben nodded dumbly.

When they had vanished into the night, Jennie Margaret began to whimper softly. It was Mr. Falloden who made up her bed on the trunk and sat beside her until sleep arrived at last; Anable was completely impotent. She sat in her chair beside the table; her lovely face was rigid, as though paralyzed by a shock. For these few moments Anable was seeing herself as if from a vast distance and her thoughts were chaotic and relentless.

So this is how it happens, she was thinking. This is reality. In what kind of a cocoon have I been living that I have never before seen shock or grief or terror? Am I nothing but emptiness, a creature of some pink and golden fairyland? I'm helpless; I'm the only one here who doesn't know what to do. I, Anable, don't know what to do.

She felt Falloden's hand press her shoulder lightly. "You're not thinking he's guilty, Anable? You're not afraid he's robbed a man?"

She shivered. "What kind of person do you think me, Falloden?"

He shrugged. "It's not a particularly queer thought. It will occur to each of us sooner or later. We'll fight it decently, but it will persist because we are very new friends and actually know little of one another."

"Those policemen," Anable said sharply. "They were dreadful."

"They were doing their duty, my dear."

She gripped the table savagely. "I don't believe Reuben has a chance," she said. "I saw with my own eyes how it is, and it frightened me. How can you be so calm?"

"You must pull yourself together," Mr. Falloden said. "This isn't like you. You're not facing reality, Anable."

She said miserably, "Do you know what kind of world I come from, Falloden? Look at me. I'm beautiful and I know the right people. You've only to look at me to know this. I've used nothing but my beauty and influence—when I want a thing I get it, Falloden, but very charmingly. Oh, Falloden, what happens to people without beauty or influence? What happens to people like Reuben? Why," she cried, "it *isn't* a bright, happy world. It's . . . it's . . ."

"Hold on," Mr. Falloden said sternly. "You're maligning yourself. You're exaggerating. You have beauty and charm, my dear, but you also have brains."

"Yes," she replied bitterly. "But what about the others, the little people with brains just as clever and creative; do they ever get the breaks I've gotten? No, Falloden, no." She stared at him sadly, her voice final and uncompromising.

Mr. Falloden wisely refrained from answering. Instead he said quietly, "Supposing you wait and see what happens to Reuben. Go to sleep soon, Anable."

"Sleep!" she cried.

"Sleep," he repeated gravely.

But only Jennie Margaret slept that night. Later, in the dawn, Mr. Falloden heard Anable open the door of the Caravan and tiptoe past his berth on the roof; he watched her cut across the fields toward Wisteria City and it seemed to him that once again her banners were flying and that she had found a purpose of her own.

He was right. Anable walked swiftly to the Western Union office in Wisteria City where she wrote quickly and efficiently:

> GEOFFREY I MUST ASK YOUR HELP PLEASE CON-
> TACT REUBEN MALONE IN GALLUP CORNERS JAIL
> HE IS INNOCENT BELIEVE ME ANABLE

When she left the office she felt better; Reuben might not have any friends left in Gallup Corners but he would have the best lawyer in Vermont to defend him.

GEOFFREY said to the policeman at the desk, "My name's Planet. I'm Reuben Malone's lawyer."

The man glanced up from his newspaper and scratched his chin thoughtfully. "Does he know about it?"

"That I doubt," drawled Geoffrey, spreading his credentials on the desk. "I've been engaged by friends of his."

"Hmm. Didn't know he had any," observed the officer. "Only one fellow tryin' to see him and outside of that nobody's asked, ceptin' a reporter or two and they don't count; vultures, all of 'em."

Geoffrey drummed his fingers impatiently on the desk. "Do I get to see him? The Grand Jury meets this afternoon, and I'd like to get started on this case. How about it?"

"I'll see if he's in," snickered the policeman, and led Geoffrey to the cells.

Geoffrey could not accurately remember Reuben. He recalled a somewhat nondescript but wholly normal boy who had spoken only a few words to him, so that when he saw Reuben now a faint look of surprise crossed his face. Away from the Caravan Reuben had lost what the last few months had gained him; he seemed haggard with the effects of despair and old.

"Hello, Reuben," Geoffrey said quietly. "Do you remember me? Miss Lea wired about you. I'm very sorry."

"Lea?" repeated Reuben blankly. "Oh, Anable, of course. Hello, Mr. Planet."

They shook hands solemnly, and Geoffrey sat down beside Reuben on the cot. "I've come to help you," he said. "I'm your lawyer now. I'm going to get you out of this."

Reuben hesitated. "They think I did it," he whispered. He buried his face in his hands. "It's just hopeless, Mr. Planet."

Geoffrey patted his shoulder. "Tell me all about it," he advised. "Begin at the beginning."

"Well, I didn't slug him. I didn't hit him over the head and steal," Reuben cried fiercely. "Why would I do such a thing, Mr. Planet? They say I ran away because I was bad; sure I ran away, but not—not with his money."

"You must go back," Geoffrey reminded him. "I must understand everything."

"I grew up in the orphanage, Mr. Planet. When I was twelve Mr. Petrie came and said he wanted a boy to help around the gas station, and he chose me. He wasn't to pay me anything for five years, just board and room, but when I was seventeen he said he'd pay me regularly. Well, I got to be a real mechanic, I did all the dirty jobs, everything I could so that Mr. Petrie wouldn't be sorry he'd taken me." Reuben's face twisted in a fight against tears. "Mr. Petrie wasn't bad. I got three square meals a day, but when I turned seventeen in May he said I was a fool to ask for a salary, I wasn't any good, no one else would want to hire me and if he heard anything more about wages he'd—he'd beat me."

"So you ran away?"

"It wasn't exactly running away," Reuben said stubbornly. "I'd served my time with him. I was free. So when I saw Mr. Peel's Caravan in back of the garage I stowed away. I fell asleep and when I woke up it was afternoon and the bus was moving. And he let me stay with them, and then Anable ran into us."

"Anable ran *into* you?" asked Geoffrey with interest.

"Yes, in the car she was in."

"Hmm," said Geoffrey thoughtfully. "That detail must have slipped her mind."

"Then we got to Virginia. That's where the police

found me. They would have found me sooner if the Caravan had gone on being a knife sharpening bus; Mr. Petrie remembered all about the muffler, you see. He remembered Mr. Peel."

Geoffrey frowned. "But why won't Mr. Petrie clear you if you're innocent?"

"He never saw what hit him," Reuben said miserably. "He was standing in his office one minute and the next thing he remembers it was night and he was lying on the floor with five thousand dollars missing."

"And you missing, too," pointed out Geoffrey. He sighed. "You picked a wretched day to leave. It doesn't take long for public opinion to jell; Gallup Corners has had two months to convict you on its street corners." He paused, absorbed in a new thought. "If Mr. Peel was here in town that same day, might he have seen anything suspicious?"

"Oh, no," replied Reuben. "I'm sure he didn't. But he's somewhere in Gallup Corners now. They won't let me see him, but he's been trying. He's wonderful, isn't he?"

Geoffrey smiled. "Quite a few people seem to think so." He stood up. "Well, Reuben, you'll be seeing a great deal of me. The Grand Jury meets this afternoon and we'll soon see what their case against you looks like. Right now I want to find Mr. Petrie and then your friend Mr. Peel."

"Mr. *Jeremy* Peel," said Reuben. "And will you tell him not to worry, please?"

"Of course," replied Geoffrey. He put his arm briefly

around Reuben's shoulders and smiled. "Take it easy, Reuben. If you've got Anable Lea on your side you can't help but win. Anable is strangely infallible."

"Well, Geoffrey," said Jeremy, leaning back in the shabby hotel rocker and placing his feet on the veranda rail, "I'm certainly glad you're here. I've been worried out of my wits about Reuben."

"Quite so," said Geoffrey. "You should be. If you've been downtown today you've heard the Grand Jury has indicted him; there is also every indication that he is guilty. He ran away."

Jeremy shivered. "But he's no thief."

"No," returned Geoffrey, "I don't suppose that he is, but that's immaterial. What I ask is, how do I get him off? Who else could possibly have done the job?"

"Stars and garters, somebody did it," groaned Jeremy.

His companion shrugged. "Mr. Petrie has listed for us the people who visited him that day. Would you care to pick a suspect from amongst them?" He pulled a sheet of paper from his pocket and began reading aloud with conscious irony. "There was Reverend Forsythe, pastor of the Green Mountains Baptist Church; Peony Haggett, age eleven, whose bicycle tires were duly filled with air; Peter Briggs, whose father would write him a check any day for twice the sum stolen; Reuben Malone, of course, and yourself. In fact, you head the list because Mr. Petrie recalls that you never paid him for the new muffler."

A look of profound surprise and disbelief had distorted Jeremy's face. He leaned forward and snatched the paper from Geoffrey's hand.

"Where's Smiley?" he demanded. "Where in heck is Smiley's name?"

"I beg your pardon?" asked Geoffrey.

"They don't have Smiley on the list!"

"Of course not," snapped Geoffrey. "Who in the world is Smiley?"

"Who's Smiley?" cried Jeremy. "Well, he was the fellow in charge of the gas station when me and Jennie Margaret came back. I paid him five dollars for that muffler. Saw him with my very own eyes and I tell you, Geoffrey, if he's not on that list of yours then he's just the chap you're after. Nasty fellow full of big talk. Claimed he was Petrie's nephew, he did."

Geoffrey's eyes were burning with excitement; "We can soon prove this," he said with exuberance, and Jeremy heard him leap to the telephone and fire a few rapid questions into it. He came back smiling. "Mr. Petrie has no nephews and knows of no one called Smiley." He sank into his chair again and regarded Jeremy with profound satisfaction.

"Start talking," he ordered. "Begin at the beginning. You're a man who's unknowingly carried a stick of dynamite in his vest pocket. You'll come in handy after all. Now give me a description of Smiley."

"He was small," began Jeremy, "well-built but small, and his nose had been broken a couple of times. His face was queer, like it was stretched tight, the skin . . ."

Hopefully, Jeremy rumbled on.

IN Wisteria City, Virginia, Anable, Jennie Margaret and Mr. Falloden lived quietly, searching the newspapers each night for some small item from Gallup Corners, and hoping for word of Reuben from Jeremy. But Jeremy was not a writing man and the post office yielded no letters from him.

"Geoffrey may write," said Anable, but she did not really believe that he would.

"It's difficult not hearing," agreed Mr. Falloden, "but we can be sure if there were good news Jeremy would let us know. These things take time."

He had started a portrait of Anable seated under an apple tree in the rich sunlight, and this was where they spent their afternoons now, Mr. Falloden at his easel with a rapt Jennie Margaret at his feet to watch the colors mould Anable's face on canvas.

"I'm tired of pretending that he'll come back tomorrow," Anable muttered. She brightened. "We didn't tell you, Falloden, but Jennie Margaret and I added seven dollars to the treasury this morning while you were buying the milk from Tim Higby. We originally went to town for bread and sugar, but we ran into a crowd of very hungry Boy Scouts."

"One of them was real cute," Jennie Margaret recalled with pleasure. "He reminded me of Lucy, all round and jolly."

Anable and Mr. Falloden beamed at each other over this observation.

"I wrote Lucy this morning." Jennie Margaret sighed deeply. "I s'pect she's almost forgotten about me by now."

"Forgotten you? Of course not!" Anable replied, but at the same time her words caused her to wonder if she, too, had been forgotten. The world moved too swiftly now for friendships; the thought made her smile all the more warmly at Jennie Margaret whose loyalties were unshakeable.

"It will be hard going back in the fall and seeing Lucy chums with someone else." Jennie Margaret smiled. "But at least I shall be close to Reuben. Reuben and I are brother and sister, you know—we made a pact."

"I'm glad you made such a pact," Mr. Falloden remarked gently. "If Reuben remembers, it must go a long way toward easing his burden."

"I write him a letter every night and remind him," Jennie Margaret announced proudly. "But of course he'd remember, anyway." She plucked a blade of grass and nibbled at it thoughtfully, her fingers busy turning the pages of Mr. Falloden's sketchbook. "Falloden," she began, "might I have this drawing of Father? It's lovely. He's not a clown here, just—just my father."

"Tear it out, it's yours," said Falloden absently, his mind now wholly absorbed with the line of Anable's brow.

They heard the rustle of pages and then a small giggle. "I remember this man, Falloden, he sold us gasoline in New York. And this woman bought ice cream from us in Tuckahoe; remember, Anable, she had twin babies?" She turned to another page expectantly. "Oh, yes, I remember this one, too," she cried, "it's me and Anable doing the dishes, only it's funny, like a cartoon. Isn't it silly, Anable?"

But she was not waiting for a reply. She said, "And this man . . ." She stopped. There was a silence so acute that Anable turned to stare curiously. "It's awfully strange," said Jennie Margaret slowly. "You have a drawing here of that ugly man called Smiley. Except of course it couldn't be him because you've never seen him. It was Father who talked to him, at Mr. Petrie's gasoline station in Gallup Corners. Only . . ."

Anable leaned over to see. She frowned. "Only what?" she asked quietly.

"Only it looks just like him," Jennie Margaret confessed apologetically. "His face looked just like an egg. Don't you remember, Anable, I saw him again at the circus?"

Anable stiffened. She was suddenly very still as though she held her breath. "This man. This Smiley," she said carelessly. "You saw him at the gasoline station *where Reuben worked?* The day that Reuben ran away?"

"Oh, yes," said Jennie Margaret. "He wouldn't let me inside the garage. All I wanted was a drink of water, but he grabbed my arm and hurt it terribly before he let me go. I didn't like him."

Anable was watching Mr. Falloden's sure strokes on the canvas. She said idly, "Was Mr. Petrie with this Smiley when he hurt your arm?"

"Oh, no. Mr. Petrie was out. But you see, Smiley was his nephew so it was all right. He told Father so."

"Of course," murmured Anable. She thought that Mr. Falloden glanced at her speculatively but he said nothing and neither did she, not for some moments, for she was busy thinking, her face entirely immobile. But after a time, as though it had just occurred to her, she glanced at her watch and gasped. "We must finish up quickly," she said. "Tonight is the evening I go to the Carnival."

Jennie Margaret and Mr. Falloden examined her curiously.

"Why, yes," she said firmly, "I'd planned it all day. Didn't I tell you? To see the fireworks, you know."

Jennie Margaret opened her mouth to speak, but Anable replied immediately to her unspoken question. "Alone," she said. "I'm going alone tonight." And she left them without a further word.

ENCHANTED CARAVAN

Once in the galaxy of light and sound, Anable headed for the E-Z Marksmanship Booth. It was the most popular and without doubt the noisiest corner of the Fair, and it was for precisely this reason that she chose it. There was new alertness about her movements now; her eyes raked the crowd coldly, as though seeking a special face, and her lips were faintly grim, as if she planned a rendezvous that was not wholly pleasing. She was, in fact, so aloof that only a few young men dared to whistle appreciatively at her although she was a vision in pale blue and white. For a few moments she lingered at the edge of the throng to watch two elderly men in overalls aim without success at the row of china ducks; as they left she hesitated, then, with a last glance around her, stepped up to the bearded man behind the counter and said, "I'd like a try. I'd like a gun, please, and a quarter's worth of ammunition."

The beard quivered as Bull's-eye Jones smiled delightedly. "Little lady," he assured her, "I'd be right proud to give you a gun, but don't shoot me. Don't shoot me, I done nothin'."

And bellowing at his own joke he held up his hands in mock surrender. "Folks," he shouted, "it's dynamite. Stick around and see what the little lady can do. A doll for the doll who can shoot the moving birds."

His audience hooted with laughter. Anable lifted her gun impatiently.

"Hey, there," cried Bull's-eye, "that's no way to shoot your husband. Let Bull's-eye show you the key-rect method."

But Anable was not to be shown; she lifted her gun, pulled the trigger again and again and shot away five moving ducks.

"Garn!" muttered Bull's-eye; he removed his hat and scratched his head. "Durned if you didn't hit 'em. Still, that was no way to shoot. 'Twas only beginners' luck. Let Bull's-eye show you."

"No, thanks," Anable said distastefully and moved from the menacing circle of his arms.

"Leave her alone," said a level voice just behind her. "Can't you see she's a lady?"

Anable stiffened; a tiny flush crimsoned her cheeks, but when she turned she was completely poised. "Why, hello," she cried gaily. "You're the hot, tired traveler who wanted ice cream!"

"In the flesh," replied the young man, immaculate now in a sharkskin suit. "Nice to see you again, baby."

"A contest!" pleaded Bull's-eye, with an eye for commerce. "A contest between the young man and the little lady. I challenge you, sir. I challenge you."

Anable gave her brightest smile to the stranger.

"You'd only lose," laughed the young man. "Me, I was born with a gun."

Leaning close to her ear he whispered, "Come on, honey, let's you and me take a powder." He grasped her arm and before Anable could protest he had elbowed them through the crowd and they were sauntering in the direction of the hot dog stand.

"The name's Charley," he told her. "Charley Jackson.

You can tell me your name or not, don't make no difference."

"Why, of course I'll tell you my name," returned Anable candidly, at the same time managing to flutter her eyelashes with delicious coquetry. "It's Anable Lea. Oh, it's lovely finding you," she confessed. "It's been so dull in this small detestable town. You being from New York, I know you understand."

"You bet," said Charley Jackson, his arm pressing closer in acknowledgment of the fact. "Spotted you right away in this crowd. Never thought I'd find a classy dish like you in this burg. Minute I got here, I thought, Great guns, Jackson, you got the bummest luck always ending up in hick towns. All these places got is one movie palace and a couple of churches." He shook his head dismally. "There ain't enough New Yorks to go around."

"We'll have to shake hands on that," cried Anable. And they shook hands, following which Anable grasped his arm so there might be no further pulverizing of her elbow. "Whatever makes you stay?" she pouted. "If it weren't for our business, we'd be miles away." She stood still and considered. "Why, you've been here for five days."

Charley Jackson winked. "A guy like me gets around. I enjoy a crowd. Never any trouble picking up money in a crowd, if you know what I mean?"

"You bet," ventured Anable coyly.

They seated themselves at the marble counter of the hot dog stand and here, under the garish lights, Anable could no longer ignore the queerness of her companion's face. She realized that once again she was staring with awe at his injured nose.

"You're cute," she said. "I'll bet you're a prize fighter."

"Ha," snorted Charley derisively. "Me, I go after bigger stakes. You think I'd soil these hands in a ring? Baby, I let others make my money for me. Then I just ease it away from them, like taking candy from a child."

Anable laughed. "Just hit 'em over the head and walk away with it?"

Charley stared at her with quick suspicion; then a light of appreciation dawned upon his smooth pink features.

"Sister," he said forcefully, "you and me talk the same language. Where you been all my life?"

Anable settled complacently on her stool and with only a minimum of effort let Charley Jackson do the talking.

THE trial had begun. Twelve quivering jurors leaned back in their hard pine seats with the knowledge their pictures would be in every county newspaper by nightfall. Sitting in their corner they were nevertheless the recipients of every attention for in their frail hands lay the future of one Reuben Malone, charged with willful assault and robbery. During the next few days they were to be flattered, cajoled, provoked and eulogized, all in the name of justice, for theirs would be the last word and their decision had the power to enhance or destroy a reputation. They were very important people.

The judge was not so concerned as they; it was a stifling August day and he knew a mountain brook where the perch swam lazily among the shallows. The district attorney, a balding, fortyish man strode nervously back and forth among his handful of witnesses. At the far side of the room sat a vengeful Mr. Petrie with a bandage over one eye that lent him a deceptively rakish appearance. Only Geoffrey seemed relaxed; he slouched in his chair with closed eyes, not from any semblance of casualness but merely because he had not slept in two nights.

The judge called the court to order briskly; the jurors were sworn in and both Geoffrey and the district attorney, whose name was Homer Todd, presented their cases.

"I shall prove," said Mr. Todd with a glance at Reuben, "that this young man cru-elly struck AND robbed his kind AND loyal employer, namely Harry Petrie, on the afternoon of May twentieth; that THIS young man diabolically planned AND carried out the robbery of a WORTHY citizen, and, with blood STILL on his hands, fled the boundaries of Gallup Corners to hide FROM the punishment due him. Ladies and gentlemen of the jury, I shall prove that Reuben Malone is THE person who assaulted AND robbed Petrie."

Geoffrey licked his lips nervously, stood up, and in much the same manner informed the jury that he would prove Reuben Malone's innocence. The jurors listened carefully to him, and the foreman nodded his head emphatically, just as he had done at the conclusion of Mr. Todd's address. Then all twelve settled back comfortably as Doctor Pettigrew took the stand. He explained the conditions under which he was called to the garage and, as the jurors turned pale with delight and horror, he described with fanatic detail the wounds inflicted and the weapon used.

"A monkey wrench," he growled. "A big one. Must have weighed five pounds."

"And now Mr. Harry Petrie," intoned Homer Todd, and the court tensed although there was not a soul among them who did not already know his heroic story by heart. "Mr. Petrie, tell the court something of your quarrel with the defendent on the morning of May twentieth," suggested Mr. Todd.

"He wanted money," stated the injured Mr. Petrie. "A salary, when I'd taken him out of the orphanage and fed and clothed him for five years! That's what the quarrel was about. And you can see he didn't wait long to get it, the young . . ."

"Objection, Your Honor," shouted Geoffrey. "The defendent is innocent until proven guilty."

"Objection sustained," mumbled the judge.

"Tell the court," suggested Mr. Todd, "the facts of the robbery, as you know them."

It seemed that Mr. Petrie owned a small safe in which he was accustomed to store a comfortable amount of cash. He bought old cars, repaired them, and sold them at a profit. He had sold two cars on the morning of May seventeenth, but had delayed his visit to the bank because he enjoyed having the money where he could see it. (The old miser, thought Jeremy.)

"It was half past three," said Mr. Petrie, lowering his

voice dramatically. "Wa'nt nobody around, so I opened the safe. Thought I heard somethin' move, but my back was to the door an' I couldn't turn fast enough. Next minute I was hit clean over the head. When I next come to it was nigh on seven o'clock in the evenin', and the sheriff and Doc Pettigrew was leanin' over me."

"And where was the defendant at the time of the robbery?"

Mr. Petrie shrugged. "Hadn't seen him since noon. He went off mad as a hornet."

"Did you see the defendant again that day?"

"No," bellowed Mr. Petrie.

"When did you next see the defendant?"

"I'm lookin' at him right now," said Mr. Petrie. "Seen him today for the fust time."

"All right," said Mr. Todd graciously to Geoffrey. "The witness is yours."

"No questions," said Geoffrey, and tried to ignore the startled glances of the court.

The fish, thought the judge, may be biting later. In fact, toward sunset—

It was unfortunate, when the prosecution had finished and Reuben was called to the stand, that he had spent the past few days in mumbling aloud his story to the walls of his cell. His words were stilted and without expression, as though they had been committed to memory, as indeed they had, and it was utterly impossible for the spectators in the rear of the room to hear but a sentence or two, which led them to feel cheated.

"Just the same," murmured a woman seated behind

Jeremy, "I'd forgotten how nice he looks. Just like any young boy. Not at all like a hoodlum."

"Don't waste your sympathy," replied her husband loudly. "See the way he hangs his head, how nervous he is? He's guilty all right. Wonder how he spent all that money."

The courtroom watched and listened as Mr. Todd arose to cross-examine.

"You had lunch at the Blue Arrow Diner," Mr. Todd was saying, "and you then walked back to your room, collected—" he paused skeptically, "collected *ten dollars,* after which you returned to the garage and climbed into the bus parked in the rear?"

"Yes, sir," mumbled Reuben.

"You did not see Mr. Petrie?"

"No, sir."

"You saw no one?"

"No, sir."

Mr. Todd raised his arms helplessly as though asking the jury to believe, if possible, such a ridiculous story.

"That's all," he said. But as he walked away a sudden thought seemed to strike him. He said, smiling faintly, "Did you have any trouble breaking into this bus in back of the garage?"

"No, sir, it was unlocked," Reuben said, but no one heard him amidst the laughter.

"Next witness," sighed the judge.

There was a change now in Geoffrey. He walked briskly to the front of the courtroom. "I should like to call Mr. Jeremy Peel to the stand," he said.

A ripple of curiosity stirred the crowd; heads were

inclined and twisted like stalks of wheat under a summer breeze. Even Mr. Todd, though forewarned, was apprehensive. Jeremy, walking swiftly, felt his heart thud and then skip a beat.

"Mr. Peel," said Geoffrey, "will you tell us your story? The court knows that you are listed as one of Mr. Petrie's customers on May the twentieth, and that it was your bus in which Reuben Malone hid. Will you tell us about the day in question and the part you played?"

Jeremy began haltingly, but as Geoffrey shrewdly accentuated Jeremy's role as key witness his confidence swelled. When Jeremy arrived at Smiley's appearance the courtroom held its breath. In the corner by the window Homer Todd's good cheer began to wilt perceptibly and he chewed on his fingers in alarm.

"And you say that he accepted your five dollars, saying that he was Mr. Petrie's nephew?"

"Yes."

"And yet this man has as yet not been mentioned in testimony?"

Jeremy nodded. The judge pulled himself together and frowned. "This is most unusual," he said.

"Indeed, Your Honor," smiled Geoffrey. "There is a most valuable witness missing. The jury cannot arrive at a just verdict without his testimony."

Mr. Todd leaped to his feet. "Can my colleague produce this witness?" he shouted. "Can you, Mr. Planet?"

"Every effort is being made to find him," Geoffrey replied. "Do you wish to cross-examine my witness?"

"I certainly do!" cried Mr. Todd, and stalked to the

stand. He glanced at Jeremy, sniffed and said, "Ah, yes, Mr. Peel. Now tell us, Mr. Peel, what is your occupation?"

"I own a caravan. We sell ice cream and candy."

"And how long have you done this?"

"About two months, sir."

"And what did you do before this, Mr. Peel?"

"I was a clown. In the circus, Mr. Todd."

"A clown? A clown?"

"Yes, sir."

Mr. Todd's grimace was so irresistibly amusing that the courtroom burst into laughter.

"Your Honor, I object," cried Geoffrey. "These are attempts to disparage Mr. Peel's profession!"

"Yes, kindly limit your remarks to the facts at issue," said the judge sternly.

"Of course, Your Honor. Now Mr. Peel, tell the jury how you happened to be in Gallup Corners last May. Is it true that you lived here some years ago, and that your daughter was born here?"

"Yes, sir. Jennie Margaret was here at the orphanage. I came to see her, sir."

"At the orphanage? Your daughter was at the orphanage? Wasn't that a bit heartless, Mr. Peel?"

"Objection," thundered Geoffrey.

"Objection sustained," nodded the judge.

"One more thing, Mr. Peel," said Mr. Todd happily. "Will you explain to the jury your relationship with Reuben Malone?"

"Why," said Jeremy, "it was just like Reuben said. He's been with us in the Caravan since May."

"You're fond of him?"

"He's like a son to me," replied Jeremy simply.

"And you would lie for him?" asked Mr. Todd slyly.

"No," cried Jeremy. "No! It's all true!"

"That's all, Mr. Peel. You may step down."

As they stood outside in the corridor during the court's recess for lunch, Jeremy said stubbornly, "You think we're going to win, don't you?"

Geoffrey's jaw tightened. "I don't know," he said. "I don't know. It doesn't look as if we shall."

Jeremy gasped. "But why? Why?"

"Because, my friend, you are the only person in Gallup Corners who seems to have spotted Smiley. You know what that makes you in the eyes of the judge and the jury? Do you know what that makes me? It makes us both liars."

"But I'm not a liar!" protested Jeremy in anger. "I'm not!"

"Can you prove it?" Geoffrey asked bitterly. "Can you bring Smiley into this court and say, Here is the man I saw? Can you give his last name, or a photograph, to the jurors? Can you prove that he even exists somewhere in the world? You can't. Even I can't be sure you saw him."

"Geoffrey!"

"That's law," he said shortly. "That's the law, and there's no way around it, Jeremy. You'll see what happens this afternoon. Under Todd's pressure even the jury will believe you to be a liar."

"And do you think I'm one, too?" asked Jeremy wonderingly. "Do you, Geoffrey?"

"I'm a lawyer," he explained impatiently. "I, too, like witnesses I can touch and see; I wouldn't be a lawyer if I dealt in abstractions. I took this case for Anable's sake. I don't want to lose it anymore than you do. It would be the first case I've ever lost."

"Stars and garters," whispered Jeremy. "If I could only find Smiley."

"Yes," said Geoffrey, "if you could only find him."

The courtroom was restless. Even the judge had lost his complacency for it had rained the evening before and his wife had prohibited his fishing because he had a weak chest. Now he chewed surreptitiously on lozenges that might subdue his traitorous cough and permit a long weekend of blissful sport.

"Reuben," whispered Jeremy, "you're all right? You aren't scared?"

"Well, yes, I am," admitted Reuben, swallowing with difficulty. "You know what they'll say. I haven't a chance, Mr. Peel."

"You've behaved mighty fine, Reuben. I'm proud of you."

"I wish I'd lied," Reuben said bitterly. "I wish I'd said I saw Smiley, too. Why didn't I, Mr. Peel? Mr. Todd just tore you apart; it wasn't fair."

"It's just everything's gone wrong," Jeremy said simply. "Everything."

"Everything's always been wrong for me," Reuben said. "All but the few weeks I was with you in the Caravan. Those days were swell, Mr. Peel. I'll remember them until I die."

"Remember?" said Jeremy. "You'll be back with us tomorrow, Reuben."

"Sure, sure," said Reuben.

The court rose as the jury filed in. The jurors moved self-consciously, aware of their responsibility and the burden it carried.

The judge said, "Ladies and gentlemen of the jury, have you reached a verdict?"

The foreman nodded severely and came forward, adjusting his glasses. "We have, Your Honor."

"What is the verdict?"

"We find the defendant, Reuben Malone, guilty of assault and robbery."

The trial had ended.

THE newspaper had cost Anable twenty-five cents and the price of a telegram, but when she returned to the Caravan with it neither Jennie Margaret nor Mr. Falloden thought to ask its price; it was both meat and drink to them to read at last about Reuben and Jeremy and the trial in Gallup Corners.

They read the Gallup Corners *Sunday Gazette* with a Virginia sun streaming over their breakfast table, and when Mr. Falloden arrived at the last sentence there were tears in Jennie Margaret's eyes.

"They weren't nice at all to Father," she said.

Anable curled her legs under her, glanced at her watch and yawned. "Wipe your eyes, Jen," she said and lapsed into stillness.

"I should have been up there, too," persisted Jennie Margaret. "I saw Smiley. Father doesn't know it, but I saw Smiley, too. I could have told them."

Mr. Falloden brought out his pipe and filled it thoughtfully. He leaned back as the first cloud of blue smoke curled into the air. "That isn't necessary, Jennie Margaret," he said lazily. "When the cards are down it is you who will have saved Reuben."

"I?" cried Jennie Margaret. "But he won't be saved. You read about it. How can anyone save him?"

She glanced up, uncomprehending, and was astonished to see that although Mr. Falloden had addressed his remark solely to her he was watching Anable intently.

"In a sense," went on Mr. Falloden, "there is a poetic justice to this. It proves an ancient maxim, namely, that no one survives alone. One lonely piece of information placed beside a small fact becomes a formidable truth."

Anable turned a suspicious glance upon him.

"Falloden, what do you mean?" pleaded Jennie Margaret. There was something here that she missed entirely; he was speaking, not to her, but to Anable, and there was a stream of understanding between them that did not include her.

Mr. Falloden's eyes were twinkling. "Think of it this way, Jennie Margaret. A strange face to Anable is but a picture seen briefly, but when another person glimpses it, a person to whom the face is known—"

A blinding light burst upon Jennie Margaret. She was horrified. "The sketch!" she cried. "It was Smiley, it *was* Smiley. And you knew it, Anable. You knew it all the time!"

"You see, Jennie Margaret," said Mr. Falloden serenely, "we have all done the best that we could, but the gods have been extremely kind. You identified a drawing by mere chance. Anable has taken up the cudgels; she has seemed very aloof these past days, leaving us alone together without explanation. Do you begin to realize where she has been, and with whom?"

"Oh," whispered Jennie Margaret, "Smiley is here, in Wisteria City, and you have been keeping him here. You didn't know, you only guessed but—oh, Anable!" She flew at Anable and kissed her. "But where did Falloden go every evening?" she asked suddenly.

Anable glanced in surprise at Mr. Falloden. He sighed. "I grew very tired of the Bijou Theater," he said. "I had hoped Jennie Margaret would not give me away."

"Bijou Theater?" echoed Anable. She gasped. "Falloden, you knew what I was up to all the time. You followed us!"

"Of course," he assured her gravely. "I could not allow any harm to come to you."

Anable glanced again at her watch and this time she smiled and did not yawn. "Jennie Margaret," she said, "you can do this. You can run to Higby's farmhouse and bring back Tim. You know Tim, who sells us our milk. He will have finished his chores and you'll catch him before he goes into town. You must bring him here. Go by the lane so that you'll not miss him."

"Tim Higby?" faltered Jennie Margaret. "But why?"

Anable's mouth tightened. "Besides being our milk-man, he's the sheriff of Wisteria City. We'll need him. It will do Reuben little good if we trap Smiley in our Caravan with only ourselves to hear. Do you understand, Jennie Margaret?"

They heard steps outside, and then a knock.

"Is it Smiley?" asked Felloden quietly.

"He's early," exclaimed Anable. "No, no, not Smiley. Not yet, Falloden. Just a gentleman called Charley Jackson who carries a car full of new luggage and remembers vaguely having seen the Caravan before."

Jennie Margaret's eyes widened. "I'll run all the way," she promised, and disappeared just as Anable opened the door.

"Come in," Anable was saying to Charley Jackson, "come in and meet my friend. There are three others of us, but they're away just now on business. This is Mr. Falloden, and he knows all about you."

Charley Jackson examined Mr. Falloden cautiously. They shook hands and withdrew to separate corners of the Caravan like wary opponents. "We going to the movies?" asked Charley Jackson, jerking his thumb in the direction of Wisteria City.

"Of course," purred Anable, "but have an ice-cream cone first. Mr. Falloden is my guardian, and he's been longing to meet you. You see, you both talk the same language." She said to Mr. Falloden, "Charley shoots a gun like nobody's business."

"She don't do so bad herself," reminisced Smiley.

"Course I been shootin' all my life, but she's good for a girl, aren't you, baby?"

"Hmmm," smiled Anable, fluttering her lashes.

"Guns your hobby?" asked Mr. Falloden politely.

"Hobby!" roared Charley, slapping his sharkskin suit at the knee. "Hobby!"

"We needn't be frightened," said Anable pointedly. "He doesn't carry his guns with him, you see."

Smiley emphasized this by shaking his head. "Never," he vowed. "When the time comes there's always something else handy. Dangerous business, carryin' a gun. Too easy for a guy like me with a temper to forget himself and go too far."

"Isn't he exciting?" broke in Anable. "Isn't it thrilling hearing all this?" She said dreamily, "Do go on, Charley, do. Don't stop. Tell Mr. Falloden the story you were telling me last night after the movies, about the time you were driving from Canada to New York and your car broke down in Vermont." She giggled. "Mr. Falloden, he just helped himself to another car. Isn't that a wonderful way to live?"

Smiley beamed at them. "That ain't all," he said. "Just between us I was out of cash, too. That's what I mean by being afraid to carry a gun. It's not smart. What's your racket?" he asked confidentially.

Mr. Falloden looked startled, but Anable said quickly, "You have such a darling smile, Charley, I'll bet your friends, your real friends, call you Smiley."

"Why," said Charley, "as a matter of fact they do."

He seemed pleased. "Now you take one time when I was in California; great place, California."

"Oh, but about Vermont," insisted Anable, "you didn't finish about the little town in Vermont. What did you call it—Gallup Corners?"

"I didn't call it by name at all," said Smiley sourly. "Listen, why you so interested in Vermont? It's all you been talkin' about since I met you." He regarded them both suspiciously.

Anable stiffened and shot Falloden a hard glance. He knew she was computing how long Jennie Margaret's trip to the farmhouse would take, and finding the time too brief—she was forcing Smiley's hand too quickly. Tim Higby had possibly been reached, but he was certainly not within earshot.

"Take it easy," Falloden said, and meant the words as much for Anable as for Smiley.

"You don't have to be so stuffy," pouted Anable. "You've been telling *me* all about your thrilling adventures, I don't know why . . ."

"This bus," said Smiley suddenly. "I said once before I'd seen it somewhere. Now where did I see it?"

"Oh, have some ice cream," suggested Anable.

Smiley got up and walked back and forth, examining the interior with a frown. "Yeah," he said, "it was Gallup Corners. There was a guy there wantin' to pay for a muffler. A little guy. Yeah, he'd have known my name was Smiley, too. Gallup Corners, where I slugged that . . ." He stopped. "You were there, too?" he asked pleasantly.

Mr. Falloden shook his head. The silence was terrifying. There was not a sound from outside. Smiley's soft words echoed like a shout; it was impossible to change the subject or talk around it. Anable's delicate timing had been destroyed, she had gone too far too early but the next words hung ripe in the air so that one or the other must say them. Falloden spoke.

"You hit the garage man over the head with a monkey wrench?"

"Yeah," said Smiley.

Now it was like a game. "And you took the money from the safe? Five thousand dollars?"

"Yeah," said Smiley, but the difference was that whereas they were delaying the inevitable he was busy thinking. It was for them a distinct disadvantage.

"And you left him lying on the floor?"

Smiley moved. "Falloden!" screamed Anable. *"Falloden!"*

"It's all right, Miss Lea," cried Tim Higby, springing through the door. "It's all right, I tell you. I've got him."

Behind him Jennie Margaret stopped to beam at them both. "We heard all about it," she said. "We busted three of Tim's milk bottles getting here."

As they brought Smiley heavily to his feet it became apparent that in the heat of the moment something other than three milk bottles had been smashed.

"Oh," cried Anable, laughing hysterically, "you've gone and broken Mr. Jackson's nose again!"

THE orchards surrounding the Caravan were thick with Virginia dust; it lay heavily upon the leaves, spilling from them in tiny clouds when touched by human hands. There was no breeze; the long purple shadows, like stains on the grass, held only an illusion of coolness. The orchards, thick with sentinel columns and roofed with sturdy limbs, served only to retain the stifling, motionless heat. There was no relief.

Geoffrey, guiding the car expertly past a litter of broken milk bottles, turned down the shady road toward the pocket of shadow that housed the Caravan. Beside him Jeremy leaned forward uneasily.

"Not a sign of life," he groaned. "Not a soul around."

Geoffrey shrugged. "Too hot. Too blasted hot for Satan himself." He wiped his forehead with one hand. "Why I ever left Vermont—"

"Well, Reuben's in Vermont," Jeremy broke in testily. "You could change places with him, you know. That is, if you wouldn't mind serving ten years in prison."

"Now, now," remonstrated Geoffrey, "we did everything we could. I've told you how sorry I am, Jeremy. You must simply try and forget the boy for a time."

"For a time!" snorted Jeremy. "Ten years? He'll be twenty-seven when he gets out, and there's no telling what jail will make of him." He felt very old, and the heat lay upon him like a suffocating hand. Geoffrey was right, of course, there was nothing further they might do, but the world no longer looked green and rich with untilled fields and sunlit pastures; a silky film lay across his vision like the dust churning beneath their wheels.

"This has been just a vacation," he said aloud to himself. "I guess we all fooled ourselves and thought 'twould last. It'll break Jennie Margaret's heart." He did not regret the flatness of his wallet, for it had been wisely invested, but he hated the sour taste of failure in his throat, the inefficiency of defeat. Life, he felt, remembering Anable, should provide happy endings to each episode that it offered.

In the Caravan, Anable heard them coming and,

throwing aside her book, she ran to greet them. "Jeremy! Geoffrey!" she cried.

Jeremy withdrew as she sought to fling her arms around him. "We failed," he said. "Reuben was like a son to me and they've sent him to jail for ten years." He walked blindly past her and into the Caravan.

"Hello," said Geoffrey, and Anable smiled at his forlornness.

"Hello, Geoffrey," she said.

He grasped her arm and they followed Jeremy toward the Caravan. "I'm sorry I didn't win it," Geoffrey said. "I've thought so much about us, Anable, that I'd—" He smiled. "I wanted to give you this case all wrapped up as a wedding present, as a stepping stone to greater things. You see, I've changed, Anable, I've . . ."

"Yes," she said.

"And as a matter of fact, there's something I must tell you."

"Of course, darling, but later, if you don't mind. Mr. Peel." She raised her voice. "Mr. Peel, there's a letter for you on the table. It came yesterday. It's from Farnum and Zailey. But first we have something to tell you."

"I don't feel like reading any letters," said Jeremy irritably. "No matter who they're from. Where's Jennie Margaret?"

"I'll fetch her now," Anable promised.

It was only a moment before she returned with Mr. Falloden and Jennie Margaret. Jeremy's heart tightened as he saw them hurrying up the path, their happiness exultant and sure.

"This is what we have to tell you," said Anable, bursting into the Caravan. "Reuben will be freed this very afternoon."

Jeremy sprang from his chair. "What?" he cried.

Anable nodded. "Jennie Margaret . . ."

"No, it was Anable," broke in Jennie Margaret.

Mr. Falloden smiled. "They freed him. We all freed him, Mr. Peel."

"But how?" stammered Jeremy. "How?"

It was such a splendid moment that it was necessary for them all to surrender to it and hug it close like a fortune, as indeed it was. They sat in chairs and on the floor, and not a sentence was spoken but that it was interrupted for further explanation and happier details.

"Tim Higby put him in jail this morning. And then he telegraphed to Gallup Corners, and they arranged a plane. Right now Smiley's landing in Vermont and *he's* wearing handcuffs—not Reuben. Tim says Reuben will be freed immediately."

Jeremy sat back and let the wonder of it play over him. He remembered what no one else could possibly know—Reuben's pale, lost face as he said good-bye to Jeremy, his eyes curiously alive and searching, as if to ask how soon he would be forgotten once the prison doors closed out the world. Reuben would be spared the ultimate disillusionment, the knowledge that misfortune was a private, lonely thing, not to be shared with others lest the contagion spread. If Reuben had sensed this at the last, he would swiftly forget it now. He had been returned to the living by the people he loved best.

But if the sentencing of a thief in a small town in Vermont was only local news, the release of an innocent boy from jail was of considerable importance all over the nation. Even as the news hummed across the country by wireless, reporters were flying to Wisteria City to interview the man they considered the hero of the occasion. They arrived before sunset, men from eight newspaper syndicates working against a midnight deadline. It was, of course, impossible to fit all of the guests into the Caravan at once, but Jennie Margaret and Mr. Falloden obligingly carried chairs into the orchard so they might entertain their guests in great style. The interview was accentuated by the toy lightning of many flashlight bulbs.

"How did you spot him?" demanded the newsmen of Jeremy. "How did you know Reuben Malone was innocent? Begin at the beginning; make it sentimental, make it homespun. You never ceased believing in his innocence? What kind of ice cream do you sell? Will you endorse it, please? Where were you born? Is this your daughter? Say something, Jennie Margaret; smile for the birdie."

They all spoke many embarrassed words which were polished later with loving care and read and immediately forgotten by millions. The reporters' pencils moved in rhythm with Jeremy's lips, like ants battling across a page. They took pictures of the Caravan, inside and out; of Jeremy smiling from the doorway; of Anable, whom they were delighted to discover, sitting in the rocking chair with her legs crossed. They presented Jennie Mar-

garet with a box of chocolates, and praised Mr. Falloden's paintings to the skies. When they withdrew, they
left behind them a litter of pencil stubs and a cloud of
cigar smoke. But it was worth it, because Reuben was
free.

"Imagine," sighed Jeremy, "Imagine having my picture in a newspaper. Now I can die happy."

Jennie Margaret planted an ecstatic, chocolatey kiss
upon his cheek. "It is wonderful," she decided, "but
don't die right away, Father."

"Of course not," retorted Jeremy. "There's too much
to do. We have to welcome Reuben home." He stopped
short. "Anable, you don't think that Petrie chap will
keep Reuben there, do you?"

She shook her head. "Mr. Petrie had his big moment
at the trial. Now that Reuben's proven innocent I hope
no one in Gallup Corners will ever forget how petty and
slanderous he was." She shivered. "If it weren't for Falloden's sketchbook—" She hugged his arm appreciatively.
"Dear, darling Falloden," she murmured, smiling.

"Hey, what about me?" cried Geoffrey.

"Why, dear, darling Geoffrey," she repeated impu-
dently.

There was a knock upon the door, and for a moment
all of them indulged in the luxury of deploring the possibility of more reporters. Mr. Falloden opened the door
and brought in a telegraph boy.

"There's two telegrams," said the boy. "Hey, which
one of you is Mr. Jeremy Peel? I want your autograph,
sir."

Jeremy grinned sheepishly. "I am," he said.

"Sign here and here," said the boy. "One for business, one for pleasure." He hung over Jeremy's shoulder while he faithfully wrote his name; then, saluting, the boy disappeared in great excitement.

"This telegram is from Reuben," said Anable. "They're flying him back here tomorrow morning. He's to arrive at seven o'clock."

"And this one is for you, Mr. Peel," she added. "Read it."

Jeremy ripped open the long yellow envelope and unfolded its message. For a moment he stared blankly at the contents. "Stars and garters, what does this mean?" he asked, scratching his cheek in perplexity. "Here's a telegram that says, 'Trust we may hear from you soon regarding offer. M. M. Turgis, Farnum and Zailey.'"

"But of course!" cried Anable. "The letter arrived yesterday when I was busy with Smiley; I put it on the shelf. You remember my mentioning it?"

"No, no."

Jennie Margaret skipped lightly across the room and opened the refrigerator. "Here it is," she announced. "I put it in here. Someone's always looking in the icebox."

They hung over Jeremy's shoulder as he scanned the letter. Its message was arranged neatly into two paragraphs, and was signed by Mr. M. Muggins Turgis.

"Dear Mr. Peel," wrote Mr. Turgis. "We have a fine opening for you here if you would care to take it. It concerns an act we are interested in developing and of course you would be the star. We are prepared to offer you three hundred a week with a long-term contract. I would appreciate hearing from you promptly about this.

"May I add, however, that I offer this to you solely upon the basis of your capable performances with us recently, and not upon your supposed reputation in Poland, since we have made detailed inquiries about your background and find that you were born in Philadelphia, Pennsylvania. My profound regards to Miss Lea. Very truly yours, M. Muggins Turgis."

"Oh, oh," cried Anable, choking with laughter. "The darling man! Mr. Peel, I'm so happy for you."

Jeremy read the letter through once again. Why, it was simply incredible; they knew all about him and still wanted him. They *wanted* him. It was the miracle of miracles.

"I can be a clown again," he whispered dazedly. "A clown with Farnum and Zailey. No more boiler rooms!"

They watched him quietly, not quite daring to move lest the spell be broken. But Jennie Margaret had something to settle.

"Does this mean—could it possibly mean I can stay with you?"

Jeremy nodded.

"I don't have to go back to the orphanage when the summer's gone?" she asked again, not quite sure.

"You'll never go back again," Jeremy said firmly. "We'll be together always. You and me and Reuben."

"Reuben, too," she breathed. "Oh, how pleased he will be, Father."

At this point Mr. Falloden, with his usual tact, withdrew to the rear of the Caravan. Accepting his hint, Geoffrey took Anable by the arm and propelled her firmly from the bus and into the orchard.

"Mr. Peel is going to cry," he said. "And I want to talk to you, Anable."

THE orchard was deliciously cool and full of purple shadows. Geoffrey steered her among the trees until they had lost sight of the Caravan, which was exactly the way he wanted things.

"Anable," he began, "I love you and I won the case after all. What's more, we haven't had a quarrel recently; we're learning, aren't we?"

"What a masterful approach!" exclaimed Anable teasingly. Then, "As a matter of fact, Geoffrey, we've

195

been too busy to quarrel; there was so much else to think about."

He leaned down and kissed her lightly on the tip of her nose. "You've been wonderful with these people," he said. "Anable, you and I are going places together; I've never felt such power in me before. Can you feel the difference? Here, touch me." He laughed as she touched him wonderingly. "Darling, I've saved and saved this good news until it hurts to keep it to myself any longer. It's—would you care to hear it now?"

Anable smiled. "When else?"

"Well," he said, "I've been offered a position with a New York law firm, Anable. Big business. Wall Street. Fame. It was offered me in the middle of Reuben's case, and for awhile I was afraid that if I lost the verdict they'd change their minds. But they didn't, and the job is mine."

Anable's smile deepened. She had almost forgotten her last intricate maneuvers concerning Geoffrey's future before she joined the Caravanners. She could have told Geoffrey the name of the firm, the salary he had been offered, and the type of work that would be his, but she wisely refrained from mentioning this.

"Of course it's wonderful, if it's what you want, Geoff."

"I've already accepted," he replied. "I've had the wrong idea, burying myself in Vermont. I've talent and brains; as you said, Anable, life is in the doing."

"Did I say that?" she queried in astonishment. "My, my! What a sententious phrase."

"Will you come back with me, darling?"

"Well, when do you go, Geoff?" she asked quietly.

He hesitated. "I'm afraid I must leave this afternoon. That's why I had to tell you now about our future, Anable. I have an appointment Monday with the head of the firm."

She frowned. "Geoff, I really must stay here. It means a great deal to me now to see Reuben come back. I shall hate to leave them, you know."

He shrugged. "I certainly don't want to risk another quarrel, darling, but aren't they rather like the friends one makes on shipboard?"

Anable sighed, and began pushing the toe of her shoe among the leaves on the ground. "Tell me about the friends one makes on shipboard," she said patiently.

"Well, they're unusually glamorous, Anable. But those friendships never last. Of course I want you to feel free to invite Mr. Peel to our home whenever you please, but I think you'll find that in New York he'll be much less interesting. There'll be new friends, new faces, quantities of exciting people."

"Yes, of course, Geoffrey, if you say so." She smiled ruefully.

They walked slowly back toward the Caravan together, arm in arm. When they reached his automobile Anable saw that it was already packed; that he had delayed his trip to talk with her. She was touched.

"You know," she said sadly, "I intended to buy you a car to replace your old one. It's been very sweet of you not to question me, but it was rather badly mangled. I sold it."

"I heard about that from Reuben," said Geoffrey, and for a moment his eyes danced with humor. "It helped make you rich, he said."

"I'll still pay you back," she said, like a penitent child. "I truly will, Geoffrey; I always pay my debts, you know. Have a good trip. I'm sorry you can't stay."

"Good-bye, darling," he said, and as he kissed her she wondered why she wanted to weep.

When Geoffrey's car had disappeared across the field, she turned moodily away and sat down on the back steps of the Caravan. With great concentration she scrubbed holes in the dust with the heels of her shoe; she felt angry inside, and sulky.

"What's the matter?" asked Mr. Falloden, sitting down beside her.

"Oh, nothing. Things are finishing up with us all, I guess."

"Yes," he said thoughtfully, "I suppose they are."

"I wonder what will happen to the Caravan now."

"Yes, I wonder, too. Funny we care."

"Is it?" mused Anable. "No, I don't think it is, Falloden. I don't want to leave the Caravan. Not ever. We've been a family in it. A warm, happy family."

"You're not sorry you came?" he asked, eying her curiously.

"Sorry?" She laughed. "You know, Falloden, when I bumped into this precious old crate of Mr. Peel's I suddenly glimpsed what it meant to him having his shabby bus wrecked—it was a matter of life and death to him. And I pitied him having so little, if you can imagine anyone pitying Mr. Peel." She sighed heavily. "All he or Jennie Margaret or Reuben wanted was a square deal from life. The chance to be happy and free." She shrugged her shoulders. "Jeremy gave them this chance, not I. Do you know what it's like not to be able to give, but only to receive? I joined them to show them a thing or two, to pay my debt and then leave. But Falloden, I discovered none of my wares were marketable in Jeremy's world. It—"

"But you did a great deal for them," Mr. Falloden reminded her.

"Oh," she replied, "I gave them a small amount of confidence, theirs was so badly damaged; and I contributed a few ideas; but you know, they ended up teaching *me* a thing or two. Do you want to hear some corn from a very modern wench?" she asked, quirking her eyebrow at Mr. Falloden. "I could try to say it lightly, but I won't; they gave me trust and companionship and respect, all the old-fashioned abstracts that have never been part of my tinsel world. I love them for it, Falloden; they're real and genuine."

"It sounds," remarked Mr. Falloden, smiling, "as though you and life are about to have a magnificent love affair. What are you planning to do with this new self of yours?"

"Circulate," she replied grimly. "Circulate and breathe fire."

Mr. Falloden laughed uproariously. "My dear, you are delightful," he said.

She gave him a heavy, brooding stare. "I don't see why you laugh."

"It doesn't matter," he apologized. "Tell me, where is Geoffrey?"

"Gone."

"Gone?"

"To New York," she added.

"I see. This is why you are looking so glum?"

Her gaze softened. "You know, Falloden, it's really very amusing; the fates have played a marvelous joke on me. Both Geoffrey and I have changed. He has become the sort of person the old Anable wanted him to be, while I—I have become someone else."

"Then you will have to set to work again," observed Mr. Falloden.

"No," said Anable seriously, "one shouldn't ever be able to change the person one loves. But I no longer love Geoffrey, anyway. Do you know, when we're alone we really have nothing to talk about?"

"I wonder if you really feel that way," said Mr. Falloden. "Perhaps in his own circle Geoffrey will shine with new light. After all, you've been moving in different groups for some time."

But Anable only shook her head stubbornly. "When I say it's no good, I *mean* it's no good." She watched a hawk circling idly over the Higby farmhouse. "Do you realize," she said, frowning, "it's I who's being left behind now? I've assumed, quite arrogantly, that I would be the first to return to my—my natural habitat. Now we are breaking up, and I am the one who is bewildered and without plans. What are *you* going to do now, Falloden?"

Mr. Falloden leaned his elbow on the step above them and stretched his long legs into the sunlight. "Vegetate," he said, "just vegetate. But I'm a stubborn soul; we started to go south, and I rather believe I shall finish the trip for us. Foolish of me, but you see, you've torn up my roots, Anable."

"Not very nice of me," she replied quietly.

"No, it wasn't."

"Falloden," she began timidly, "Falloden, I'd like to go south, too."

He shrugged. "You do not as yet know what you want, Anable."

"Yes, I do," she insisted.

"Then what is it that would make you happy?"

She hesitated. Then she said, "You, Falloden."

"What are you talking about?" he asked quietly.

"Us," she admitted shyly, blushing. "I've loved you very foolishly for some time now, Falloden."

His face was turned from her so that she could not know how he received this outrageous confession, but when he at last looked at her he was utterly composed but for a gay twinkle in his eye. "My dear," he said, "if you do care for a man who is neither successful nor brilliant, then you are indeed foolish."

"So you're going to turn me down," she said hotly. "Falloden, I deserve it, but couldn't you be kinder?"

201

She blinked her tears away furiously. "You don't believe it's the real thing, but I'm bitterly afraid you're wrong. No, I haven't missed a wink of sleep and my appetite has been splendid but I feel lost, and in pieces without you. I was sure we'd be so very, very happy. Oh, Falloden, what shall I do now?"

He said gently, "You might marry me, my dear. It has often occurred to me that we would be extremely happy together."

"You mean you do love me?" she cried.

"Of course," he replied, and as he moved down to her step Anable was swept with a dizzy weakness that she had never before experienced at the approach of a man. "I'll wire Geoffrey in the morning," she whispered as Falloden took her firmly into his arms—a moment later and Geoffrey had ceased to exist.

The Caravan was dim as they entered, hand in hand. Jeremy had forgotten the lights; he and Jennie Margaret sat in the cabin of the bus talking earnestly of many things. Jeremy started when he saw them. "Stars and garters," he said, "it's late. It's dark. Time to light up."

He moved across the room and one by one the lights sprang up under his fingers, immersing the Caravan in cozy warmth, lingering richly in the red curtains, and highlighting the copper kettle. "It's good to be home," he said. "I'll miss our old Caravan."

Anable said, "I'm going to be married, Mr. Peel."

Jeremy shook his head and blew out the match.

"That's no surprise," he said, and lowered the wick on a lamp. "That's no surprise at all."

"Well, I'm surprised," cried Jennie Margaret joyfully. "I thought you and Geoffrey would never get together. Now, with you married, and Reuben free at last—" She stopped and caught her breath. "Anable, did I tell you? It's going to be better than an adoption; Reuben and I are going to a regular school and live in an apartment, and Father's promised to buy me a bicycle. Say you'll come and visit us, Anable. Father says Lucy may visit us every Christmas. And you must, too, Anable—you and Geoffrey."

"But what about Mr. Falloden?" asked Anable mischievously. "What about poor Mr. Falloden? Aren't you leaving him out?"

"Oh," whispered Jennie Margaret, very conscience stricken. "Oh, dear. Father, it's true—what will happen to Mr. Falloden?"

Mr. Falloden cleared his throat. "As a matter of fact, Jennie Margaret, several matters have been newly arranged since I last saw you. I, too, am going to be married."

"You?" thundered Jeremy.

"You?" repeated Jennie Margaret unbelievingly.

"He's marrying me," explained Anable. "Me."

"You? You and Falloden?"

Jeremy sat down in the nearest chair. "This isn't a joke?" he asked suspiciously.

Mr. Falloden shook his head. "No joke."

"Well!" gasped Jeremy. "This is the biggest surprise of all!"

"Surprise," echoed Jennie Margaret. "It's a *confusion*."

"You and Falloden, eh? What happened to Geoffrey?"

Anable smiled. "He just didn't measure up, Mr. Peel. Not with Falloden around, you see."

A tiny smile illuminated Jeremy's features. "I kind of like the idea," he said. "Understand, it startled me a wee bit, but it's a fine idea. What do you plan to do?"

"It doesn't matter," Anable replied softly.

"You've got no big plans, Anable?"

She grinned. "I don't need any big plans. I've got what I want, Mr. Peel, and you can't tease me any longer."

This was true; it was necessary only to look at them both to see their contentment. It was pleasing to Jeremy, who had found many qualities lacking in Geoffrey.

"You maybe wouldn't want the Caravan?" he asked suddenly.

"The Caravan!" gasped Anable.

"I'm thinking," said Jeremy, "that I won't be needing the Caravan anymore, and I'm also thinking you and Falloden might be able to use it. Go to Florida, maybe, like we planned once."

"Oh, Mr. Peel, that's wonderful of you," breathed Anable. "Why, there will be plenty of room for painting in here, and I can sell ice cream."

"You'd do this for us?" asked Mr. Falloden, staring deeply at Jeremy.

"I'd do more," murmured Jeremy shyly. "Mind you,

I haven't gotten over my surprise yet, but I should have seen it for myself." He smiled. "The Caravan has surprised us all."

Jennie Margaret hugged Anable impulsively. "Isn't it wonderful?" she cried. "Now we can really live happily forever after, can't we? Like all the fairy tales I've ever read!"

There was no one to disagree.

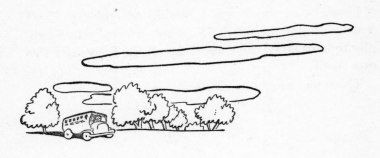

IN the dreaming stillness before dawn, Jeremy and Jennie Margaret made their last trip in the Caravan. At their left, down in the valley, the green and white lights of the airport gleamed like jewels under water. There was a pleasing hint of autumn in the air, and from the trees came the shrill conversation of the birds as they made their morning's ablutions. Jeremy beamed contentedly; at the back of his mind lay the knowledge that at that very moment Anable was preparing a picnic breakfast in the orchard—there would be bacon and eggs, flapjacks and honey, and quantities of steaming coffee and cool milk—a breakfast fit for kings.

"I like early mornings," Jennie Margaret said with satisfaction, her face as bright as the sky. "They give you a magic feeling, like anything at all might happen."

Jeremy smiled, his eyes on the gray road that unwound before him, his touch firm on the wheel. In the west he could see a sliver of moon as it drew closer to the hills; presently it would vanish to give way to the sun.

"Just like us," he thought solemnly. The Caravan would disappear soon with Anable and Falloden, and each of them would go their separate paths. The Caravan had served its purpose.

"The mornings will never seem so magic again," he said to Jennie Margaret, sighing faintly.

"I don't believe that," replied Jennie Margaret wisely. "Why, this summer has been just the beginning. For *all* of us."

And this was true. But what if there had been no Caravan at all? The thought returned to Jeremy as it had haunted him on many other happy occasions. He thought of all the people in the world who had never found, or dared to find, a way to break from the dismal circle of their lives; of people who still lived in ignorance of the richness, the love they might find waiting for them just around the corner. The Caravan had been only an instrument for their needs; when it lay rusting in a junkpile its spirit would, nevertheless, prevail. Alone, none of them would have triumphed.

As the road turned into the highway it seemed to Jeremy that the dawn sharpened and clarified itself, so that all things held an emphatic beauty that he had never before noticed. It was as though they moved in a dream and, dreamlike, he saw before him the world, the only world which he had ever known, a world of separate, lonely human beings continually reaching toward one another, eternally banished from sharing by the fear of refusal, of humiliation, of distrust.

"But stars and garters," he cried out, and in his anger brought his fist down upon the horn so that Jennie Margaret jumped at the noise. "We're all human. We're all lonely. We need each other. *We need each other.*"

Over the mountains from the north came the sound of a plane; in a moment they saw its riding lights, brilliant like Christmas stars.

"Oh, Father, it's Reuben's airplane," cried Jennie Margaret, sitting erect. Her eyes shone with anticipation.

In the east the sun emerged to stripe the field with gold. Jeremy parked the Caravan by the gates of the airport and they walked out, hand in hand, to greet Reuben.

THE END